The Big Hello And The Long Goodbye

Peter Gessner

HILLIARD HARRIS

HILLIARD HARRIS

P.O. Box 275
Boonsboro, Maryland 21713-0275

The Big Hello And The Long Goodbye Copyright © 2007 by Peter Gessner

First Edition-April 2007
ISBN 1-59133-199-4
978-1-59133-199-5

Book Design: S. A. Reilly
Cover Illustration © S. A. Reilly
Manufactured/Printed in the United States of America
2007

This book is dedicated to the memory of my parents, Doris Lindeman and Robert Gessner

ACKNOWLEDGMENTS

The twin stories in this book are, of course, fictional. They are nonetheless inspired in part by real incidents. Some years ago, a young woman was murdered by her fifteen-year-old brother in what appeared to be a tragic ritual killing: she had apparently violated the strict moral code of her Middle Eastern immigrant parents by engaging in pre-marital sex with a local young man. The case attracted little attention at the time—the motive and killer were known, and few felt the need to look further. Although I did not work on the case, I knew the detective who was hired by the boy's attorney and who went on to ask the right questions.

While employed at a well-known San Francisco investigative agency, I found myself assigned to tail a man who engaged in random one-way conversations with telephone polls. This individual had earlier discharged a shotgun in a private driveway, and delivered credible threats to a prominent local family. On the day a member of this family was to address a large public gathering near the waterfront, the man boarded a bus headed towards the event only to disappear at the end of the line. Fortunately the event went off without incident. Sometimes reality is gentler than fiction.

The author would like to thank, in no particular order, the following individuals who read the manuscript at different stages in its development: Sterling Lord, Patricia Holt, and Thomas Farber encouraged the author to do his best work. Others whose direct or indirect encouragement helped me stay the course include Stephen and Kathleen Gessner, Jamie Wolf, Nancy Mattingly, Sandra Sutherland, Joe de Francesco, Corrine Usher, Mary Zawacki, David Sullivan, Jeanette Strasser Falk, and especially my daughter Francesca Gessner, whose lawyerly skills and logical mind saved me from more than one glaring misstep. A special word of appreciation is due "Tony," the Palestinian proprietor of my neighborhood convenience store, whose passionate discussions of the seemingly intractable divisions in the Middle East prompted me see his corner of the world in sharper focus. I hasten to add, however, that the novel's perspective on those troubles are my own and not Tony's.

Last but far from least, I owe a significant debt to those colleagues with whom I trained and worked, and whose skills, sophistication, and good humor transformed what had once been a shadowy profession operating at the margins of respectability into one worthy of wider recognition. A core group of San Francisco private investigators like the late Hal Lipset, Beverly Axelrod, and Joe Barthel, as well as Jack Palladino, David Fetchheimer, and Melody Ermachild, redefined the standard of care through their work on a series of challenging cases like the Jonestown massacre, the first Michael Jackson child abuse case, and the Unabomber murder trial. Because of these men and women, San Francisco private detectives are presently regarded as among the best in their field.   Their presence and example help ground this transplanted New Yorker in his adopted home.

PROLOGUE

Sheets of gray fog pour through the Alemany Gap, blown east by a stiff wind coming off the Pacific Ocean. Along the neighborhood's main artery, a few headlights move like paired fish in an underwater aquarium past closed burrito palaces, used car lots and second-hand furniture stores, their plate glass windows pebbled with condensation. This unloved corner of the City—known to urban planners as the Excelsior District and to cab drivers as the Deep Mission—is shut down tight for the night.

Along a nearby side street, a single porch light carves out a patch of lime green color from the façade of a modest stucco home. An older Detroit muscle car pulls to a stop. Dual exhaust pipes rap and throb as the driver throws the big engine into neutral. A tall, thin, young woman with dark hair dressed in the evening clothes of her generation–black slacks, short black jacket and black thick-heeled shoes–steps lightly to the curb. The driver–older, hair cut short on top with a short rat's tail trailing over the collar of his leather jacket–moves to her side, and in one motion pulls her to him. A soul kiss, a not too discreet grinding of pelvises, and the girl turns toward the stairs. The big car throttles up and pulls away, leaving a thin trail of blue exhaust.

As the girl climbs the stairs, the remnant of a smile tugging at the corners of her mouth, one hand raised to straighten her hair, a figure emerges from the darkness under the stairs. The porch light spills on a face, freezing it: a young man, mocha skin, perhaps Middle Eastern. He moves purposefully forward, a human snowplow, both arms extended in front of him, hands clasped as if cutting the air. The light glints on the shiny silver 9 mm automatic held between his hands. The girl half turns in his direction; the hands and gun are close now. She raises her left hand as if to stop this inexorable forward motion. The gun bucks and leaps three times. Pale flame and smoke stab at her. She crumples down on the steps.

Three long seconds before lights snap on inside. The boy–for now it is clear he is really no more than fifteen at most–moves up the steps and enters the house. A middle-aged man in a bathrobe appears in the hall; behind him, a gray-haired woman peers from a door she has cracked open. The boy walks up to the man, hands him the gun butt-first and continues down the hallway. The man, his face etched with pain, looks from the fallen body to the boy's receding back. The woman, keening and wailing, moves past him toward the motionless girl. In the middle distance, a siren rises and falls.

CHAPTER ONE

Walker woke to the soft rolling motion of the earth. *Goddamn California*, he thought at once. A digital clock told him it was 5:30 AM, and he knew he would not be able to go back to sleep. Faint sunshine probed the slats of his Venetian blinds. As Walker, wearing only a tee shirt with the words "Coming" lettered across the front and "Going" across the back, padded slowly to his window to look out over the San Francisco Bay. His gaze took in the Alcatraz searchlight, now almost redundant in the growing dawn light, as a pair of oil tankers slid with slow majesty toward the Richmond refineries across the Bay in the distance. Walker, a transplanted New Yorker, found even small earthquakes unsettling–how were you supposed to know whether the little ones were Nature's benign release of pent-up forces or harbingers of much worse to come. He came to believe that even native San Franciscans could not tell the difference.

Moving now by instinct in the half-light of his studio apartment on the eastern slope of Telegraph Hill, Walker entered the kitchenette, found and filled a dented saucepan with tap water, and placed it on a gas ring. He poured ground coffee from a bag reading "Peet's French Roast" into the pan and lit the gas jet. He shed his tee shirt, and tossing it toward a pile of what appeared to be other discarded garments in the corner of the room, loped naked toward the walk-in shower stall. The sharp needles of warm, steamy water felt good on his shoulders. Walker stood motionless, silently taking inventory. Edging toward his mid-fifties, his body seemed reasonably firm, and had succumbed only partially to age and gravity. His brown hair was not unpleasantly flecked with gray, and his face, marked by high cheekbones and pale gray eyes, was tan and unlined. Shoulders hunched, Walker leaned languorously against the fiberglass shower wall. Locked and tensed muscles began their slow tectonic release. He felt the water wash away the residue of fatigue from the night before, long hours spent hunkered down in a rental car with binoculars, a bottle of Martel brandy, and an empty milk container for his bladder, waiting for something to happen.

His skin now a glowing pink and encased in a large, fluffy beige towel bearing the emblem of the St. Francis Hotel, Walker stood in the kitchenette carefully pouring his version of "camp fire" coffee into a thick earthenware mug. He managed this operation with one hand, only a few grounds finding their way into the mug, while his free hand adjusted the volume of a small transistor radio. He listened for a moment to the day's traffic and weather—*stop and go on the deck of the bridge, metering lights on, fog in the morning, burning off at noon.* Walker thought: they should have this on tape by now. He approvingly took his first restorative sip of caffeine.

Walker knew that at his age he couldn't take many more assignments like the one he had been on the night before. It was what was known in the investigative business as a loss prevention gig—cable installation technicians were thought to be walking off with expensive optical and platinum wires and allegedly stashing them in outdoor lockers at a suburban rental facility. Walker spent three successive nights watching those lockers. By the third night he found himself hallucinating, convinced that the dwarf-like light stanchions in front of the lockers were Spanish conquistadors in full battle dress. Fortunately, no one had appeared. Walker reminded himself that the assignment was a favor to a fellow investigator who had to attend his daughter's graduation from high school, but in truth was it had been a slow month and bills were pilling up. A larger worry gnawed at the margins of his consciousness, a fear that the phone would stop ringing and the cases would become more routine and less challenging. He hoped that the stake out of the rental lockers had been an aberration, not an omen.

By now, the oil tankers had become smudges on the horizon. The morning sun was shining directly into the room and Walker lowered the blinds. When he first saw the "For Rent" sign on the stucco pre-war apartment building in a narrow alley off the precipitous Filbert Street steps, he almost balked at the cramped space and dilapidated fixtures. Of course, he wound up being seduced by the rent-controlled lease and the million-dollar view. He was told by the listing broker that he was fortunate: "Some people pay extra to get an apartment with a view—you're getting a view with an apartment thrown in." Walker immediately hired workmen to redo the plumbing and strip the floor to bare wood, which he varnished himself over one long weekend. The apartment felt snug and trim.

Walker moved toward a small flash of blue in an oval glass bowl. Archie, an Indonesian Beta fighting fish, had entered Walker's life without warning as a gift from a woman he had recently met. Like the fish, Linda Massingale was new, over-bred and high-strung. The ex-wife of a society lawyer, she lived in a Russian Hill penthouse but knew the cheapest restaurants in Chinatown as well as the precise times of art-house twilight movie matinees. Walker was not sure if she was a keeper or potential trouble.

When he first met Linda, Walker thought of Raymond Chandler's admonition to Philip Marlowe not to go to bed with someone who has more problems than you. Despite his admiration for Chandler and the mystery authors whom Walker often binge-read late into the night, he found himself unable to follow the famous author's advice—teenage lust overwhelmed him whenever he was in Linda's force field. Walker tried to tell himself it had been the car and not just the woman: after all, the first thing he saw was the fire engine red 1953 drop-head Morgan roadster, stranded on the approach to the Golden Gate Bridge, and only when he pulled over did he see the long legs, slender hands, and quick smile. By then it was clearly too late. Walker consoled himself with the thought that unlike the detectives in mystery novels, he was always drawn to slow cars and fast women. Or was it the other way around? He was never sure.

Archie broke the surface of the water to take his morning food pellets from Walker's fingers. The radio announcer talked about a pit bull attack on a child in the East Bay. This morning's earthquake was hardly mentioned. In recent months it seemed that the local airways had been dominated by stories of road rage directed against lap dogs or the fatal mauling of a beautiful track coach by attack dogs owned by a husband and wife lawyer couple. *All animal, all news, all the time*, Walker thought.

Despite his thirty-plus years in the City by the Bay he still considered himself an outsider living on the edge of America. A native San Franciscan, Linda reminded Walker— her hand walking on two fingers down Walker's back as they lay in bed earlier in the week—that the continent sloped to the west, and everything not rooted or tied down to something eventually rolls towards California. Thinking back to his own westward migration several years after the Summer of Love, Walker knew there was truth to the joke. He wondered if Linda had meant him. He was strangely afraid to ask.

Pleasantly recalling the light pressure of Linda's fingers, Walker contemplated Archie for a long moment through the thin corkscrew of mist rising from his steaming coffee cup. According to information Linda had found somewhere on the Internet, Indonesian fighting Betas spent much of their time creating chains of air bubbles for the female to use as egg incubators. They would do this even in the absence of a female Beta, confident in a biological imperative that somehow, somewhere, sometime, the Great Wheel of Nature would turn and provide them with a mate. Indeed, this morning, unperturbed by the movement of the earth, Archie was eagerly pushing bubbles around the edge of his bowl like a logger breaking a logjam. Moving closer to the bowl, Walker mouthed the word "hopeless" in Archie's direction, at the same time letting his hand drift to the answering machine.

Walker's fingers moved liked a jazz pianist on the buttons as he sped through a solicitation for a "free" weekend at Lake Tahoe, slowed for a moment to catch the words of a court clerk informing him that a file he had ordered from storage was now available, and the voice of Jake Jacobson, college roommate, now corporate lawyer, wanting to talk to Walker about a missing person case. "Top-drawer, I kid you not, call me pronto," the familiar voice intoned. Walker smiled, remembering Jacobson as a man of free-flowing hyperbole who underneath was a grown-up Holden Caulfield, ever poised to catch falling lambs as they went over the cliff. Still, there might be something there, and besides, the rent and his annual investigator's license fee loomed in the next week.

The final message was from Malcolm Delucca, a former rock musician who had, a decade ago, adapted to changes in music tastes and the *zeitgeist* by reinventing himself as an attorney. Delucca had graduated at the top of his law school class, boasting he'd never met a fellow student or professor. (He took all his classes on the Internet.) He quickly rose within the criminal defense bar, and two years ago ran for a vacant Municipal Court judgeship, losing by a whisker-thin margin. "I got us a homicide, Companero," Delucca's deep tenor intoned. "Outer Mission Palestinian family killing. I'll be in my office all day..."

Walker, still moving slowly and deliberately, slipped on his wide-wale corduroy slacks, a blue chambray dress shirt with button-down collar and his weathered leather jacket. He selected a muted silk tie from a twisted and tangled pile, ignoring several with swirling bold patterns at least a decade out of fashion. Downing the last of his coffee, Walker used his free hand to shovel his pager, cell phone, and reporter's notebook into his over-the-shoulder brief case. He unhooked the chain lock on the front door and stepped out into the morning light.

CHAPTER TWO

Walker left Telegraph Hill and walked down the steep part of Montgomery Street until it fell into the flat gridiron pattern of the city's financial district. Although he owned two cars—a late-model, generic black Japanese sedan and a British racing green 1956 MG convertible—he often preferred to move around the City on public transit.

Reaching Market Street, he boarded one of the outbound vintage streetcars the city ran during the summer tourist season. Walker gazed out his window at the morning tide of tourists, men and women on their way to work, and street people. He particularly liked the mix of old and young who gathered, rain or shine, near the foot of Powell Street to play chess at makeshift card tables. All ages, forms of dress, and ethnicity seemed to be represented—Walker noticed homeless people sitting opposite men in business suits; punkish teenagers across from matronly women; here and there a single person bent over the table, focused and intent.

Walker left the streetcar and crossed to the waiting trolley bus that would take him to the Potrero neighborhood. Awkwardly weaving and dodging the elbows and packages of middle-aged Asian women who boarded with him, he glimpsed for a fleeting moment a remnant of a much younger self, the North Jersey scholastic all-American high school wide receiver he had been. *A legend in my own mind,* Walker told himself. Finding a seat, Walker, his tall Caucasian head poking above his fellow passengers', felt the bus glide away from the curb.

Powered by overhead electric wires, the ride was serenely quiet. As the bus moved through the South of Market neighborhood, Walker noticed auto repair shops and garment warehouses where Internet and Multi-Media companies once dotted the landscape. Most of the remaining riders on the bus were Asian women who left in small clusters, heading toward cramped lofts where clothes were sewn at piece rate.

Walker got off at 16th and Bryant Streets, the former site of Seals Stadium, the prewar Pacific Coast League ballpark, once a showcase for the younger incarnations of national heroes Joe DiMaggio and Casey Stengel. The stadium— existing for Walker only in archival pictures—had been replaced by a large anonymous shopping center and underground garage. Walker crossed the street toward a faded three-story building on the corner. The top two floors consisted of offices, while the ground level was taken up by a bar and restaurant known as the Double Play. The name was a clear reference to its once famous neighbor, but Walker liked to think it also evoked dual offerings of food and drink. He and Linda often ate there when they felt the urge for hamburgers served on sourdough bread, or fresh calamari. Walker mounted the steep flight of stairs next to the bar entrance and entered the office of Malcolm Delucca.

The outer hall boasted redwood wainscoting and a checkered marble floor that Walker guessed dated from the turn of the past century. A faint mustiness hung in the hallway and Walker speculated that the building must have gone up before the advent of air conditioning. Delucca shared the suite with three attorneys and a receptionist/secretary who came in three days a week. Walker moved past the empty reception desk and tapped lightly on a frosted glass door panel. Without waiting for a response, he pushed the door open.

The room was cool and dark. The attorney had closed the blinds, effectively blocking out the shopping center. Walker guessed Delucca did not want to be reminded every day of the desecration of the old ballpark. He knew that Delucca was a big baseball fan—the game was in his blood, he often said—and he regularly took his young son to Giants games in the new downtown ball bark.

Delucca, in shirtsleeves and a brace of red firemen's suspenders, kept his sun-streaked blonde hair at almost the same length it had been when he played bass guitar for one of the Bay Area's premiere rock groups. A talented performer and composer, Delucca had learned by trial and error to handle the band's contracts, and quickly discovered he had a talent for what he later came to call 'lawyering.' The degree that eventually permitted him to practice before the state bar hung proudly on the wall next to the group's single gold record. Delucca soon lost interest in codicils and moved with vigor into the murkier but never placid waters of criminal defense. In the past fifteen years, he had become a skillful player in what Walker thought of as the criminal justice food chain. Delucca was both respected and feared by opposing prosecutors. More importantly, his clients liked him: he had a reputation as a tough battler and a fair man.

The attorney motioned with one hand for Walker to sit in the visitor's chair.

"Our guy will be here in a few minutes," he began. "His name is Hussan Bakkrat. He and his family run a convenience store in the Mission. You probably read about his son Ali in the *Chronicle*? The one who killed his sister?"

"These days I just try to read the sports section," Walker replied. "Everything else is too painful."

"You need to broaden your horizons."

Delucca opened a folder on his desk. Walker saw a typed police report, released to the defense as part of a process known as reciprocal discovery during which both sides perform a careful dance of show and tell. "The girl...Noor Bakkrat...was coming home from date with her boy friend when it happened. She lived with her family on one of those streets off Geneva and Mission."

Once Irish and German working class, Walker knew that the neighborhood was now home to many new arrivals from Asia and South America. And more recently the Middle

East. He pictured trim lawns, small stucco homes, pale pastel colors.

"The boyfriend...Benjamin Navarro...Hispanic male, mid thirties, expensive leather jacket, rat's tail hair cut...drops her off in one of those Detroit muscle cars, a red Nova or Impala, nobody in the report knows which." Delucca, glancing at the report, continued. "The girl...gets out, kisses Navarro goodbye, and starts to climb the stairs. Her brother, Ali, is apparently under the stairs...holding a nine-millimeter. Neighbors and the father hear three shots. Before the father can open the door, Ali walks in, hands him the gun butt first and goes inside and sits down on the family sofa. The grandmother, who also lives there, goes crazy, starts wailing. Someone— looks like a neighbor—calls 911. The cops arrive. Ali just sits there on the sofa, not a peep from him."

Delucca closed the folder and slid it across the table to Walker.

"This is your copy."

Walker thumbed the pages. He guessed there were maybe a total of fifteen. Most homicide reports he had seen ran to twice that at least. He looked up at Delucca.

"Anything to tie him to the nine, other than that he handed it to his father?"

"Beyond that his prints were all over it?"

"Yes."

"They bagged his hands, tested for gunpowder residue."

"And?"

"Positive. For a change, the crime scene techs played it by the book."

"What about the boyfriend—Benjamin? They test his hands?"

"They tracked him down couple hours later. His test was negative. You'll find the report in the supplemental section."

Walker tilted his head at the attorney.

"Yeah, I know," Delucca sighed. "This is a real winner. A regular whodunit."

Walker thought: not a lot of loose ends to explore. Maybe not. There was always more.

"Has the boy said anything to you?"

"Jesus, Walker." Delucca smiled.

"No harm in asking." Walker smiled back. He knew that in order to take on a case, a defense lawyer need not know the answer to questions of this sort. Sometimes he would be more effective not knowing.

"It seems that Ali didn't like his sister dating this Benjamin guy," Delucca said. "The whole thing begins and ends there."

"Didn't like? That could well be the understatement of the year."

"Look, this Navarro guy is older, somewhat on the flashy side and plus he is non-Islamic. His dating the sister was an in-your-face kind of thing. Pretty natural the kid would hate him."

"If that's true, why didn't Ali shoot him? Why shoot his sister?"

"Don't forget that double standard thing in those countries—you know, men can screw around all they want, but when a woman does, it is a great dishonor."

"I know. But still."

"The kid isn't talking at all. That's the first thing I want you to do, go see him at the Hall and see what the hell his story is," Delucca continued.

"It could be some kind of fundamentalist religious thing."

"Damned if I know."

A polite tapping on the door prompted the attorney to rise from his seat. Delucca ushered in a tall man with salt and pepper hair, light caramel-colored skin, perhaps in his early fifties. Hussan Bakkrat's dark double-breasted suit was expensively tailored and fit him well. He stepped into the room with quiet composure, his features a mask of grief.

"Mr. Bakkrat, this is the detective I have hired to help us."

Bakkrat took Walker's hand in a firm grip. Walker noticed that his hand was slender, cool. Bakkrat stared intently at Walker.

"Mr. Delucca was very highly recommended to me," Bakkrat said.

"You are in good hands, Mr. Bakkrat," Walker replied.

Bakkrat sat down in a chair next to Walker. His baleful eyes took in the office furnishings, coming to rest on the gold record. Working his face into a smile, his gaze came back to Walker.

"Is he as good as the famous Perry Mason?"

"Better," Delucca responded. "Not all my clients are innocent."

Bakkrat's smile flickered for a few seconds and then went out. "My son, Ali, is a good boy. He studies hard at Lowell High School. He is on the chess team. This tragedy makes no sense."

"How did he get along with your daughter, Mr. Bakkrat?" Walker asked.

"Oh, they were very close. Always very close. He worshipped Noor. They were very close."

"Is there any reason he would want to hurt her?" Walker continued.

"None at all...none."

The room grew quiet. Walker waited, allowing the silence to take hold in the room. He and Delucca both knew that people, like nature, tended to fill a vacuum where one existed.

Bakkrat finally spoke.

"My son is so young. Surely they will take that into account?"

Delucca drummed his fingers lightly on the desk.

"We can't be sure at this point, Mr. Bakkrat. We will do everything we can to see that the District Attorney charges your son as a minor. But I must advise you that a judge can rule that he should be tried as an adult."

"What does that mean?"

"It could mean first degree murder, Mr. Bakkrat," Delucca replied. "Twenty-five years to life in state prison." He paused and chewed his bottom lip. "Worst case, they could charge a special circumstance. Lying in wait."

"I don't understand."

"The way the law is currently written, there are a half dozen so-called 'special circumstances,' which allow the state to ask for life without possibility of parole. Lying in wait is one of them."

"My God," Bakkrat whispered.

"Given his age, I doubt they will go that route," Delucca continued. "But we have to be prepared for the worst."

Bakkrat struggled for a moment to regain his composure.

"I am sure you will both do your best," he said in a low voice.

"Can you tell us something about your family, Mr. Bakkrat?" Walker asked.

"Whatever would be helpful, yes of course," Bakkrat responded. "I was born in Ramallah, Palestine. I came here in 1983 to join a cousin who had a small grocery store on Cortland Avenue. Ali was born here. Noor was the eldest and she was born in Palestine. My wife and I worked hard, perhaps too hard. We were not always able to supervise their development."

"In what way, Mr. Bakkrat?" Walked asked.

"We are not very religious people, Mr. Walker. But our land and culture are very important to us. Even here. Especially here. Both children love America, which has been very good to us. But sometimes they forget where we come from. I did not always know whom they were seeing or who their American friends were. But perhaps a father in this day and age is not supposed to know these things."

Bakkrat paused and looked at both men for confirmation. Walker responded with what he hoped was a smile of encouragement.

"Do you know the boy Noor was with the night it happened?" Walker asked.

"She had been seeing him for a little while," Bakkrat replied. "I hardly knew him. I think he worked in a garage in Daly City."

"We will need to talk to him."

"His name is Benjamin Navarro."

"How did Ali and this Benjamin get along?" Walker continued.

"I don't know...you will have to ask him."

"Was there any animosity? Friction? Words?"

"There could have been."

"If you know about something between them, this would be the time to tell us," Delucca prompted.

"I can't say, really," Bakkrat hesitated. "There was perhaps jealousy, perhaps the feeling from Ali that this boy was not good enough for his sister. I had that sense, yes."

"Do you know where Ali got the gun he used that night?" Walker asked gently.

"I have no idea. We have never had a gun in the house."

Once more a silence settled into the room. Delucca looked at his watch.

"Gentlemen, I'm due in court in forty minutes," he announced.

Bakkrat rose and handed Walker his business card, asking to be advised of the progress of the investigation. The door closed behind him.

"It's Chinatown, Jake," Delucca said, scooping papers into his briefcase.

Walker moved to the window and lifted one of the blind slats. He tried to estimate the distance of one of the young DiMaggio's home runs, but realized he did not know the original location of home plate. He found himself thinking of Tolstoy's famous suggestion that all successful families are successful in the same way, while the ones that come apart find their own unique ways to fail. Walker wondered what the failure had been in the Bakkrat household. He guessed it was his job to find out.

"Bring me some mitigation, Walker," Delucca said, already moving to the door. "Otherwise, we're dead."

Walker let the blind fall back into place. He speculated that DiMaggio's blast might have reached Pets Unlimited, if home plate had been where the video rental outlet now stood. Walker turned and followed Delucca out the door.

After parting from Delucca on the street, he headed directly to the pet store. Inside, Walker averted his eyes as he passed an aisle of "feeder fish" swimming listlessly in their containers. Living food. As he bought a packet of pellets for Archie, Walker thought: *Aren't we all.*

"You mean to tell me you were *at* the goddamn store and didn't buy a female companion for Archie?"

"I'm not a matchmaker. I'm a detective."

"It's heartbreaking to think of him making all those bubbles for nothing."

"We live in an imperfect world, Linda."

The long nose of the Morgan pointed toward Japan as Walker and Linda Massingale sat thigh-to-thigh in the sports car's narrow bucket seats gazing out at the incoming ocean swells. They were parked on the westernmost edge of the continent, in the lot of the Beach Chalet, a restored W.P.A.-era building with red Spanish roof tiles built over a series of graceful sandstone arches. Fronting the Great Highway and the Pacific Ocean, it was now a popular restaurant. Walker and Linda found the food indifferent, and on the way had stopped at a deli to provision themselves with a fresh sourdough baguette and soft goat cheese.

Linda broke off a piece of bread, spread some cheese on it, and guided it to Walker's mouth. The sun was a pale disk behind the late afternoon fog bank. Defiantly, Linda had dropped the Morgan's top. She was dressed in a white cotton blouse, tan slacks, and spaghetti-strap sandals. To ward off the chill, she draped an open cardigan sweater over her shoulders. Walker liked the way she looked.

"How would you like to spend your *entire* day in a cup?" Linda said, refusing to back off.

This was a sore point between them. In the early days of their relationship, Linda had maneuvered Walker to Pets Unlimited, and while he was gazing absently at flea collars, she arrived at the cash register with a small plastic pouch undulating with water and a solitary Indonesian fighting fish soon to be known as "Archie." Handing the clerk her credit card, Linda explained to Walker that this fish would kill other males and had to be kept separate. "He was in this tiny cup, and I rescued him," she said matter-of-factly. In her other hand she held a small bowl containing a handful of gravel from which protruded several packets of food pellets. Walker consented to baby sit the fish for a few days, but under no circumstances would he be responsible for its care and well-being beyond a few weeks. "Come on, Walker," Linda responded, flashing her most winning smile. "It's a fish. The epitome of low maintenance."

Walker wanted to say that she was becoming the epitome of high maintenance, but held his tongue. Archie—named by Linda after Nero Wolfe's legman—had lived with Walker now for the past six weeks, and although fed regularly, was not particularly loved. Walker knew that their "argument" about Archie and his unanswered paternal expectations (those endless bubbles) was not a metaphor for anything: Linda, in her forties, with two grown sons, had let him know clearly that she was not interested in more children of her own. Still, Walker feared Linda saw Archie as a small chunk of the universe capable of breaking up the stark austerity of his apartment. Although not opposed to less austerity in his personal life, Walker simply wanted to have his fingers on the spigot, controlling its flow. Linda, on the other hand, liked to impose change on her surroundings. When she wasn't working as a part-time counselor at an inner city public school, she made phantasmagoric animal forms in the weekly community college ceramics class she religiously attended. A few weeks back, Linda had presented Walker with a black, glistening shark whose teeth looked like a sharp picket fence. He had no idea where to put it. At first he tried his nightstand, but quickly became uncomfortable waking each morning with those fierce teeth mere inches from his head. A few days later, he'd placed the shark next to a plastic water plant at the bottom of Archie's bowl.

The wind was coming up and Walker reached back and lifted the canvas top over their heads. In the sudden quiet, they stared and locked eyes. Walker's mouth found Linda's lips. Drew her tongue into his mouth, felt his toes curl, and then they came up for air. Linda tilted her head, inclining it back toward continental America and the City. Walker smiled and turned the key, and the Morgan's throaty engine caught and fired.

CHAPTER THREE

Walker found himself cocooned in a bed of fog as his dark green MG left the freeway and coasted down a long hill into Daly City, San Francisco's suburb of stucco homes and marginal businesses. Over the years, Walker's visits to this bleak neighborhood of identical post-war bungalows had left him empty and spent. He thought of Malvina Reynolds' song "Little Boxes," inspired by these same unending rows of tract homes. Walker read somewhere that country singer and Rhodes Scholar Kris Kristofferson, born in Texas but who had grown up in nearby San Mateo, experienced a nameless fear every time he passed the little Tinker-Toy houses.

For Walker, each visit to this small, fog-shrouded coastal municipality prompted withdrawals from his already depleted bank account of psychic energy. On a strictly practical level, Daly City was a virtual Bermuda Triangle for delivery truck drivers and detectives from the big city—streets named Alta Vista Way bisected Alta Vista Drive and Alta Vista Court lurked at the next corner. It was a potential nightmare, and he found his eyes repeatedly darting toward the Thomas Brothers map that lay open on the seat, the location of Benjamin Navarro's garage circled in red Magic Marker.

Next to the map and jammed between the little sports car's bucket seats lay a fat Manila envelope. Like most private investigators he knew, Walker often worked several cases at once, and tended to use his car as a moving office. The previous evening, with one eye on a playoff basketball game on the tube, he sifted and sorted through scraps of paper, photographs, smudged envelopes sent by messenger to his apartment by his old college friend Jake Jacobson. For reasons he did not pretend to understand, Walker believed that fracturing his attention this way often paid off months later when an apparently lost paragraph, a face, or a string of facts rose magically to consciousness. He found the technique useless when it came to retrieving   misplaced house keys or reading glasses.

The packet of materials Jacobson sent Walker concerned a high-tech entrepreneur whose brother had gone missing in San Francisco. Alan Singleton, an accomplished mathematics professor, was feared by his brother to be bipolar and possibly self-destructive. David Singleton insisted that Jacobson use an investigator who was near his brother's age. "Alan was part of that whole sixties thing," Singleton explained to Jacobson. "He may try to see people from that era, so it would help if your investigator had some familiarity with the scene." Jacobson made an appointment for Walker to meet with Singleton later that night at his hotel to discuss the case.

The garage appeared without warning on Walker's right. Large open bay doors gaped like hungry mouths, and steel hydraulic lifts thrust upwards toward the roof like giant chrome teeth. Walker saw several cars and pick-up trucks perched on the lifts, their wheels hanging. One of the open bays had apparently been converted into an improvised paint shop. Walker caught sight of a young man methodically sweeping a spray gun across a fifteen-year-old Chevrolet Impala. A single dark ponytail hung down the back of his blue coveralls, his face obscured by protective goggles and a cloth mask.

Walker continued past the garage, up a short incline and parked. He sat still for a moment, his fingers drumming absently on the teak dashboard. Walker wondered if the place was a chop shop, a temporary home for hot cars on their way to new owners not overly concerned about lineage or legal title. He got out, locked the MG, and walked down the hill toward the garage. The hiss of the paint gun became louder, sibilant and insistent.

Walker stood in the doorway of the paint bay and watched the wand deposit an even mist of black lacquer over the Impala's rear quarter panel. After almost a minute, the man looked up and switched off the machine, instantly transforming the wand into an inert metal rod. He appeared to be in his late twenties or thirties, with a thin sharp nose and a muscular body encased in paint-spattered coveralls. Walker noted that the ponytail was cinched by a rubber band.

"Help you?"

"Benjamin?"

"Who wants to know?" Eyes wary. The goggles pushed aside now, the mask pulled down below his chin.

Walker fished his laminated P.I. license from his wallet. Benjamin Navarro glanced at it with complete lack of interest.

"So?"

Walker put his license back in his wallet and sighed. He smiled at Navarro. No response.

"Noor's father hired me," he began.

"You're working for the bastard of a brother who killed her," Navarro said, wiping the dripping end of the paint wand with a soft towel.

"That's right," Walker answered. "I thought you maybe could help me understand what happened."

"Why should I?"

"No reason," Walker replied. He walked over to a barrel and picked up a card of paint swatches and appeared to study it intently.

"I don't have to talk to you," Navarro said, his feet planted wide apart.

"That's right. You sure don't," Walker said. He waited, continuing to thumb through the swatches.

"Noor and I had planned to get married. I bet you didn't know that."

"Did Ali know?"

"She was going to tell him and the old man, but she was afraid. I told her I'd go with her when the time came."

Navarro looked toward the door and the traffic moving outside. Walker put down the swatches and turned to Navarro.

"When did you first meet Noor?" he asked.

"Six months ago at Caesar's, you know the big salsa dance place near Army Street?" Navarro returned his gaze to Walker. "She was there with some friends from her office. I asked her to dance."

"What happened then?"

"We were together every week after that. She liked to dance, she loved going out to salsa clubs late at night. She was, like, blossoming out, you know, blooming—you could tell she had all this pent up energy." He paused, fingering the paint wand. "I really loved her, man."

"Did she talk about her family, about Ali?"

"Not a whole lot. She let on that they were pretty conservative."

"Did that include Ali?" Walker asked.

"That's why this whole thing is so fucked, man," Navarro responded, gripping the wand tighter. Walker noticed a homemade tattoo on one forearm, the kind often made by convicts in prisons. "She always talked about Ali as being special, the real smart one in the family," Navarro continued. "The one who played chess and everything, the one who was going to go to college and make something of himself. Then he goes off the deep end and does this...this crazy fucked-up thing."

"Did she ever say that Ali had told her to stop seeing you?"

"If he did, she never talked about it," Navarro continued. "But I know that she always wanted me to pick her up and drop her off at her house, and I was never invited inside. Looking back, I wish had been. Maybe I could've prevented this."

"What do you think set him off?" Walker asked.

"No idea, man. Must have been some fucked-up Arab thing. I hope he fries for it," Navarro spat out, his teeth tight, almost clicking together.

"Ever been in trouble with the law yourself?"

"What business is that of yours?" Navarro looked down at his tattooed forearm.

"It's easy enough to find out."

"I was in C.Y.O. for auto boosting. That was a long time ago."

"How long?"

"Three years and seven months."

"Clean since?"

"Yeah. You can check."

"Had to ask—I got a job to do."

Navarro turned on the compressor and the paint wand began to vibrate.

"Yeah. I know. Getting murderers off. Some job."

He pointed the wand at some newspapers spread on the floor and turned on the nozzle. Paint hissed into the newsprint six inches from Walker's leather Timberland moccasins.

"I got a job to do, too," Navarro shouted above the noise, swinging the wand smoothly back toward the Impala.

Walker looked down at his shoes, now flecked with a fine mist of paint. Drawing his breath in a long slow sigh, he walked out of the bay and hiked back to the MG.

Walker exited the freeway at Seventh and Bryant Streets and made a half-left past the Hall of Justice. He knew the jail would be locked down in twenty minutes and no visitors would be let in while the deputies made their afternoon head count. Walker scanned nearby alleys for scarce parking spaces, then circled the block for five long minutes, cruising past bail bond offices, parked police cruisers, and lawyers hurrying up the broad steps past street people and jurors. Trusting that his middle-aged peripheral vision could pick up the flash of car keys—a twentieth century urban talisman indicating some pedestrian was about to become a driver—he finally sighted a place in a narrow alley a block from the Hall and slid in behind a large truck.

Walker retrieved his Sheriff's Department-issued jail ID card from the glove box and was starting to walk back toward the Hall when he noticed, double-parked two car-lengths ahead, a dusty brown van with bald tires, not moving and with no back-up lights or turn signals flashing. A very tall man emerged. In Walker's mind, there was no question this person could dunk a basketball in any pickup game in this or any known universe. Striding closer on pipe-stem legs, the man leaned down to glare at Walker. Everything about him suggested big-time trouble.

"That was my space," he said evenly. Black leather pants and a lined and creased face, Walker noted. He guessed the man to be on the far side of his forties.

"Well, I'm not a mind reader."

First paint on my shoes, now random fucking road rage, he thought.

The man stepped closer. Instinctively, Walker's right hand went to his pocket and came up holding the jail ID card. He brought it close to the man's face, hoping that the Sheriff's emblem would give Leather Pants pause.

"Back off. I don't have time for this."

"Think I give a shit that you're some kind of investigator, you little fuck?"

Abruptly and without preamble, Walker felt hands close around his throat. Thumbs pressed on his Adam's apple, his throat constricted as air left his lungs. Walker tried to summon the muscles of his lower back and thighs, to marshal them into an upward kick in the direction of the man's groin, but it seemed to take a long time for the message to reach his leg. Walker felt the grip on his neck tightening. His chest burned. Suddenly, he heard a sharp voice to his left.

"Hey, motherfucker, leave that man alone." A stocky black man with gray iron filings flecked in a thick wooly head of hair addressed the man in leather pants. "That ain't your space. You got no claim to it."

Leather Pants loosened his grip on Walker's neck and turned to look at the new arrival. Despite his uniform of homelessness—ill-fitting pants, torn leather jacket, an empty Wendy's soft drink cup in his hand—this man radiated a presence.

"You want to fight somebody, you fight me," he calmly informed Leather Pants.

Leather Pants eased away from Walker. He knelt next to the MG's front wheel and retied his shoe.

Another man, this one white and fiftyish in a black beret with stubble on his face, wearing a tattered army jacket and dirty plaid pants that puddled at his ankles, appeared next to the black man. "Yep. I saw it too," he said softly, his hands resting loosely on the handle of his brimming shopping cart. He stared hard at Leather Pants.

"Sure, no problem." Leather Pants finished tying his shoe and stood up. His face muscles had gone slack.

Walker, sucking in great gulps of fresh air, glanced at his watch. The jail would be locked down in eight minutes. He turned toward the first man.

"Thanks. I mean it."

"No problem, man."

Walker went into his wallet for a twenty-dollar bill.

The man chuckled, reached forward, and the bill vanished in his fist.

"This is my block. I watch everything that goes down here."

Walker offered a second five dollars to the man in the army jacket, who held up his hand in refusal and backed away. "Just calling it the way it is."

Walker smiled and turned up the sidewalk. In a moment, the new jail building loomed ahead, its rounded surfaces and mirrored windows in stark contrast to the cold slab monolith of its neighbor, the Hall of Justice.

Christ, I impersonated a peace officer back there, Walker told himself. *Risked my license. For what? To be a hero?* In Walker's moral calculus, if anyone had been a hero in the encounter, it had been the homeless guy, because he'd decided not to be an observer. It was his street and he applied his code of asphalt justice to the situation precisely because swift, certain truth was crucial to his own day-to-day survival. As the song said, if you live outside the law, you must be honest. The guy in the army jacket seemed to know that, too. Walker showed his ID card to the sheriff's deputy on the main gate and went inside.

CHAPTER FOUR

Walker sat hunched over a scarred table across from Ali Bakkrat. Occasional shouts and random clanging metal doors pierced the quiet of the small, cave-like interview room, reminding Walker of the soundtrack of World War II submarine movies. *Run silent, run deep.* Even in this newly-built modular lockup dubbed by some as the Glammer Slammer because of the $30,000 designer couch and abstract art in the front lobby, Walker felt submerged, underwater, as if an enormous weight pressed down on him.

Prisoners were segregated and appropriately color-coded by the severity of their offenses: orange jumpsuits for misdemeanors and some felonies, red for violent crimes. In the greenish light leaking from fluorescent fixtures in the ceiling, Ali's jumpsuit appeared almost wine-colored and his bare forearms were unnaturally pale. He was shackled at his feet and a waist chain pulled his handcuffed wrists snugly into his body. Walker realized that Ali had received the treatment generally reserved for those whom society deemed the worst of the worst: adult men who killed.

The young man's soft brown eyes looked downward at a small object Walker guessed might be a piece of gum or an eraser that he kneaded between his fingers. The wispy hope of a mustache marked his upper lip.

Walker slid his business card across the table, pinioning it to a sudden a stop with his forefinger inches from Ali's hands.

The boy glanced at the card and then back at whatever held his attention.

"I'm here to help you," Walker began.

He withdrew his finger from the card. No response.

"Anything you tell me is confidential," Walker prompted. "It goes nowhere but to your lawyer."

"No, thank you," came the reply. As if he were refusing an offer of an item on a restaurant menu so foreign it would not be worth trying.

Walker sat for a moment listening to the metal and human sounds of the submarine. If he let it, he knew that it could become white noise, washing out all other sounds. Walker could not begin to imagine what it would be like to be in the submarine for months, let alone years. What judges and lawyers called LWOPP—Life Without the Possibility of Parole—seemed to Walker the true definition of cruel and unusual punishment. The gas chamber was finite. The LWOPP submarine was an unending journey with no homeport. Ali's fingers continued to knead the object he was holding. Walker reached across the table and plucked it away. The brown eyes shot up, glaring.

Walker held in his hand a small piece of bread shaped like a horse's head. Turning it over, he saw a penny wedged into the pliable dough forming a base or pedestal. He placed the piece upright on the table and smiled.

"Not bad. Nice, in fact."

Ali remained silent.

"I figure they wouldn't give you real pieces," Walker continued. "They'd worry somebody could rub or grind them into sharp points to use as shanks." Walker held the piece to the light. "Definitely serviceable." He handed the object back to Ali.

"They let me have an old checkers board," Ali said. His voice was muted and Walker had to lean forward to hear better. "The knights and the bishops I made from the bread. I used chewing gum for the rooks and the king and queen."

"What about the pawns? You had to make a lot of them…"

"That was easy. In the day room, they have construction paper. I used a hole punch and collected the little circles."

"Like confetti."

"Yes, like confetti. I made stacks and glued them together." A small smile creased Ali's face.

"What did you use for glue?"

"My saliva."

Walker grinned back. At least he's looking at me, he thought.

"I invent games for myself," Ali continued. "No one in the day room can play chess. They just play checkers. You know chess?" Ali's eyes were unwavering, on Walker now.

"Some. It's been years. You know Jose Capablanca?"

"Of course." A small smile of disdain creased Ali's face. How could Walker dare suspect that he might not recognize the name of the great Cuban chess grandmaster?

Walker stood up and pushed back his chair. He punched a button on the wall that rang in the guard's station.

Ali's eyes followed Walker.

"You're leaving?"

Walker did not reply, his attention focused on an approaching guard. "I think I have the Capablanca book at home," Walker said, letting his gaze swing back to Ali.

"It's been out of print for years." The voice marveling, excited now.

"I'll bring it next time."

The guard appeared at the door. Walker watched Ali rise from his chair, pluck the business card from the table, and move with shuffling small steps out the door and down the long corridor. Walker felt the boy's eyes on him as he moved off in the other direction. An iron door clanged somewhere.

Up periscope, Walker thought to himself as he walked out the main gate.

Showered and shaved, his good Harris Tweed jacket and dress slacks more or less pressed, Walker stepped from the still-moving California Street cable car at the crest of Nob Hill across from the Fairmont Hotel. The city fell away on four sides, and an early evening sparkle of lights blinked from the hills. Seven hills, Walker reminded himself. Just like Rome. Of course, there were far more than seven, but somehow over the years that number had worked itself into guidebooks and handouts from Chamber of Commerce. The sight of winking lights on the surrounding hills never failed to check Walker's breath. In the distance, down the steep California Street grade, the steel girders of the Bay Bridge glinted in the dying light of the bay.

The Fairmont's spacious lobby had the heft and feel of an elegant nineteenth century bank lobby or an Edwardian men's club. Marble columns soared above a thick, embroidered carpet, and an unseen trio of musicians worked a variation on a famous show tune Walker recognized but could not name. He made his way along an avenue of miniature palm trees nestled sedately in large ceramic urns and descended a broad staircase to the downstairs bar.

The bartender nodded as Walker slid onto a corner stool and ordered an Anchor steam beer made at a local brewery a few blocks from Delucca's office. Walker was pleased when it arrived forty seconds later without the irrational accompaniment of an unwanted wedge of lime he encountered in all too many bars. At this early evening hour, the clientele consisted of a smattering of patrons: a tourist couple at a nearby table dressed in what local columnist Herb Caen used to call the "Full Cleveland" (sweatshirts, plaid Bermuda shorts, baseball caps); a middle-aged professional type in a dark blue suit with tastefully thin chalk-white stripes at the bar, a cellular phone pressed to his ear; and, further down the polished surface, a burly, fiftyish man was nursing what Walker guessed was a whisky sour. His dark hair, white at the temples, was swept back into what in an earlier decade would have been called a D.A. Expensive designer bifocals hung from a chain around his neck and rested on a pastel-colored cashmere sweater. Walker hesitated for a moment and, beer in hand, moved across the soft carpet toward him.

"Mr. Singleton? David Singleton?"

"You must be Walker," the man replied, his face breaking into a broad smile. "Let's grab a table."

Walker followed Singleton to a pair of comfortable wing back chairs in the corner of the room. Seated, their drinks in front of them on a small marble-topped table, Walker spoke first.

"I wasn't sure I had the right person. You know, you look a little like the guy who owns the pro football team across the bay."

Singleton emitted a throaty chuckle.

"Yeah, I get that a lot."

Walker returned Singleton's smile and studied the man's face for another moment, fighting to shake the notion that he had seen Singleton or someone like him recently. After a moment, Walker decided he must have watched too many football games on TV and the resemblance between this new client who wanted his brother found and the famous renegade sportsman was purely coincidental. Jacobson had advised him that Singleton was wealthy, but reclusive. Singleton owned neither an apartment nor an office, at least outwardly. He opted instead to commandeer a large suite on the Fairmont's top floor to serve both functions.

"You're probably wondering how a man loses track of his own kid brother," Singleton began. "We grew up in Manhattan and spent summers on a lake upstate near the Canadian border. We lost both our parents when I was twelve and he was eight. After that, we were raised by relatives and sent to different boarding schools."

"That must have been difficult for both of you. How did it happen?"

"An accident at our summer house. A fire. My brother and I were away swimming in the lake when it happened."

"A terrible thing. My sympathies."

"Yes, well, we move through and beyond what life deals us. For a while, it brought Allan and me together. Then, as we got older, we drifted apart. He always was a loner while I was the social one. In college, he was a brilliant math student. Made some theoretical breakthroughs that are still talked about in the professional journals. And not only there, mind you. Computer industry types took a long look at him. I went another route entirely. After college—and the obligatory stab at being an actor in some very obscure off-off Broadway plays and a year spent in Europe sitting in cafes drinking brandy and looking sullen and ascetic—I came home and floundered around some more before I went into business for myself. One thing led to another, and I became what for lack of a better description, a junk bond trader. Now I own several of the companies whose bonds I used to hawk."

Singleton's smile suggested he enjoyed the irony.

"What happened to Allan after college?"

"He received a prestigious appointment in the math department at Cal," Singleton continued. "But something was changing. He said the world was hell bent on self-destruction and he didn't want to go down with it. He experimented. Joined Zen meditation groups. Lived on a commune in British Columbia. Somehow through all this he always kept in touch. Cal held his position for him, they always welcomed him back. Then the notes started coming a couple of months ago. Really frightening and disturbing notes."

Singleton paused and sighed.

"In a way I feel responsible for his disappearance."

"How so?"

"He always wanted my attention and approval. Maybe by disappearing and writing these damn notes he thought he'd finally get it. You've seen them?"

"Yes," Walker replied, recalling the thick packet he had received from Jacobson.

"Mostly gibberish, I'm afraid. I worry that he's had a psychotic break of some kind. I want him found before he hurts himself—or someone else. Here, look at this..." Singleton handed Walker a sheet of cheap lined notebook paper filled with a dense, handwritten scrawl. Walker scanned a few sentences and looked up at Singleton.

"It seems to be some kind of rant against Harrison Bledsoe," Walker said. To Walker and other Bay Area residents, Bledsoe was a household name, first associated with the invention of the grommet studs that held together the canvas pants of many a Gold Rush miner and whose descendants now stood at the head of one of largest privately-owned multinational apparel companies in the world.

"Precisely," Singleton nodded emphatically. He motioned for Walker to continue reading.

For several more minutes, Walker waded through long, serpentine sentences describing the financial and human havoc Bledsoe caused the people of the world. The diatribe concluded with the words "This three-legged shark, his mates, and his whole gang must be eliminated from the forward progress of history."

"I like a man who can turn a phrase," Walker remarked, placing the paper aside.

"I take it seriously, Walker."

"I didn't mean to suggest that I don't. Have you thought about going to the police or the F.B.I?"

"Christ, Walker. Look at Waco...Ruby Ridge. I don't want my brother killed."

"I understand. It's just that they have the manpower and resources to find him."

"Remember the explosion in Madison back in the sixties that killed some poor bastard who was studying late at night in the university's math building?"

"Certainly." The event had made national headlines. The bomber was never found or prosecuted.

"Allan was a math major at Madison in the late sixties," Singleton said, retrieving Allan's note and putting it his coat pocket. "Even though he didn't have anything to do with the explosion, that whole business will come up again if I give Allan's name to the feds. And give them an excuse to use deadly force when and if they find him."

Walker nodded. He thought of his own FBI file, which he had leveraged out of the government some years back under the Freedom of Information Act. It was little more than the times and dates of anti-war and civil rights meetings and marches he had attended as student. Enough to put him on a Watch List, nonetheless.

"What makes you think Allan is in San Francisco?"

"Several things." Singleton dug into his pocket again. "First, because this last batch of letters have all been postmarked from the City." He handed over a packet of letters to Walker. "Secondly, because Bledsoe is located here. And lastly, because this is where I live. As I told you before, I think he is pleading for my attention."

Walker glanced at the postmarks and put the envelopes down on the tabletop.

"I know, this whole thing must seem fairly hopeless," Singleton smiled, swirling the melting ice cubes in his drink. "But you have one rather major factor going for you, Walker."

"And what might that be?"

"I think my brother wants to be found."

"Why do you say that?"

"Because this last batch is peppered with clues...here, let me show you." Singleton selected a letter from the packet. "This is from last month. He goes on at some length about getting new glasses at a place that had good espresso coffee a block away...and here in this one he says here that he is living in a bank vault, but it is very comfortable and has great scenery. What do you make of that?"

"I don't know, Mr. Singleton. Maybe in Allan's world it makes perfect sense." Walker scooped up the letters and slid them into the side pocket of his jacket. "On the other hand, after I go down to the Building Department and look through old permits to remodel bank buildings into residences, I might be able to tell you something."

"This should also help you," Singleton said, handing Walker a slip of paper. "An eyeglass prescription made out to someone named Ollie Drupt. Unfortunately, the name of the prescribing optometrist is illegible."

"Ollie Drupt sounds like the name of some children's TV program. Or else it's made up. I might do better cross referencing optometry offices with nearby cafes and see what shows up."

"Fine. Do your best. That's all I can ask. He is my brother and I want him found. Here's your retainer. "

Singleton slid a thick envelop across the table toward Walker, who opened it and saw a crisp packet of hundred dollar bills. He did a quick count: thirty.

"I trust it's sufficient," Singleton said.

"More than sufficient, Mr. Singleton." Walker placed the envelope in the breast pocket of his jacket. "You understand that payment is for my efforts, not results."

Walker produced a small receipt book, flipped open the pale blue cardboard cover, wrote something and tore of the top copy, which he handed to Singleton.

"Of course." Singleton accepted the receipt without looking at it and rose from his chair. "I completely trust Jacobson's evaluation of you."

"And what was that?"

"That you were tenacious." He held out his hand. "I like that."

Walker stood up to shake Singleton's outstretched hand. He felt Singleton's envelope shift slightly in his pocket.

A soft hiss eddied at Walker's heels as he went out the hotel's brass revolving door. In the distance, the necklace of lights on the surrounding hills glinted with a metallic brightness that seemed almost as empty and unforgiving as his assignment. *Give me the needle and I'll find the haystack,* Walker comforted himself.

CHAPTER FIVE

Walker turned on his computer and slid Miles Davis's *Witches Brew* into his tape deck. The late morning fog hung in thin threads above the glassy surface of the Bay as Walker watched a brace of ocean-going container ships slide past Angel Island a long rifle shot away. Linda, freshly showered and wrapped in Walker's oversize bath towel, methodically cast hamburger shards onto the top surface of Archie's miniature universe. Walker frowned until Linda reminded him that the small blue creature was a carnivore and *liked* the occasional piece of flesh. With a quick shrug of his shoulders Walker turned back to the computer screen. Linda bent her head forward and languidly swept a har dryer across dark strands of wet hair.

Walker was neutral on the issue of computers. Other P.I.s either swore by or mocked them. For Walker it was simply a tool, one of many. Like the snub-nosed .38 Detective Special that sat in a locked case in the back of his closet. This particular handgun was no longer a weapon of choice for most modern law enforcement agencies; it had been replaced by lightweight automatics with greater stopping power. Walker, however, religiously continued to oil and clean the gun, and liked the way it felt in his hand. He seldom carried it, and refused to own a shoulder holster. In his personal moral universe, a gun was a tool of last resort.

Walker slowly and deliberately picked his way through a series of public records databases, looking for electronic footprints of Ollie Drupt. As he expected, the name did not turn up among those citizens who contracted national movers, or subscribed to magazines or owned real estate in the state of California. The screen asked him if he wanted to search watercraft and airplane licenses. With a click, he declined. Mr. Ollie Drupt, a.k.a. Allan Singleton, did not seem the type who would tool around in motorboats or do figure eights in piper cubs. Walker's fingertips beat out a quick tattoo of frustration on the desktop.

He opened another database. A dozen articles in math journals by or about Allan Singleton came up. The earliest appeared to date from Allan's days as a graduate student. Most were technical; some were in German. Walker ignored them and entered David Singleton's name. *Know your client*, he told himself. Unsurprisingly, there were numerous hits in business journals and publications. Speed-reading through the lead paragraphs, Walker learned that the success of Singleton's original privately-held company was based largely on the discovery of cutting edge computer operating codes. The net worth of Loon Lake Ventures had vaulted to the mid seven figures in two years, and had remained there, despite the collapse of other technology sector stocks. Walker closed the screen and shut down the computer.

Next, he studied two age-enhanced sketches of Allan that David Singleton had given him and that Walker had thumb-tacked on the bulletin board next to his desk. The first depicted a clean-shaven man in his late forties with chiseled features and penetrating eyes. In the second image, the eyes were watery and blurry behind granny glasses, the hair long. Allan's pointed chin was covered with a full, tangled beard.

The dryer stopped. Walker noticed that Linda had begun to sift through Allan Singleton's notes to his brother.

"I think Archie needs a friend badly, Walker."

"Abstinence builds character," Walker responded, staring at the sketches. Why hadn't the artist split the difference and produced one with, say, hair the length of Mick Jagger's? *Everything is either/or these days, no shades of gray anymore*, Walker thought.

"No, I mean it," Linda continued. "He almost bit my finger off when I was giving him the hamburger."

"That doesn't mean he's horny," Walker replied. "Just means the little fucker can't tell the difference between cows and humans."

He reached for his San Francisco reverse telephone directory. It was a thick, heavy book, and anyone over forty would be obliged to squint at the cramped print, but Walker found it more reliable than its internet cousins, which he feared were only sporadically updated.

The hair dryer started again. Walker opened the book, and after some rummaging in his desk, found a magnifying glass. He carefully wiped it clean with his shirt tail.

"For the love of God, Walker."

"What?"

"Don't you look the veritable Sherlock...where's your plaid deer-stalker hat, the one with earlaps?"

"Don't mock an aging gumshoe."

Walker glanced at the list he'd compiled earlier of downtown espresso bars and compared it to a second list he'd made, this one of optometrist offices. Leafing back and forth through the directory, he carefully cross-referenced the two lists.

"They multiply like goddamn rabbits."

"Not without a partner they don't," Linda answered.

"No, I meant caffeine emporiums. It's almost as bad as Seattle."

Walker determined that there were at least six possible locations where one could sit with one's coffee and have an unobstructed view of an eyeglass store. Some were giant chain outlets, others were designer boutiques. Fortunately, all the likely candidates were in the Financial or Union Square districts, within walking distance of one another. However, to canvas them would still take the better part of a morning, Walker realized.

Linda looked up from Allan's notes and frowned.

"These are pretty weird, Walker."

"The notes? I know."

"Did he give you everything?"

"I assume so. Why?"

"A couple of them refer to other notes that I don't see here."

Linda shook off the towel and stepped into a champagne-colored slip.

"I assume he gave me what he thought would be useful," Walker responded. He left his desk and disappeared into his closet. "I was hired to find the guy, not to analyze his literary output."

He emerged wearing a dark blue Pendleton wool shirt and wide-wale corduroy slacks.

"I've got to jump on it. If you don't find a missing person in the first couple of hours, you know that it will wind up taking days or weeks. It's some sort of cosmic rule."

Linda gave him a quick kiss on the cheek. She was dressed in a button down blouse, a straight skirt cut to below the knee, and sling-back heels.

"We all make our own rules, Walker," Linda said over her shoulder as she headed towards the door.

"Wait…"

"I have an afternoon meeting. See you at Sam Woo's for dinner. Bye, darling."

In a moment she was gone, the door clicking shut on what looked like bright sunshine. Walker sighed and turned up the volume on Miles Davis. He sat again at his desk and wrote a check to the Bureau of Security and Investigative Services in Sacramento for his biannual license fee, slid it into a stamped and addressed envelope, licked the flap, and closed it. He took out a yellow felt-tipped marking pen and began to highlight the names on his list of optometrists. Several moments later, he was humming to himself, half a bar behind Miles.

A sally port clicked open when Walker pressed his ID card against a smeary control room window and once more he was on board the Big Submarine. He tried to shut out the atonal symphony of shouted voices and clanging doors as he approached the interview room. Ali looked up and smiled briefly. Walker sat down opposite the boy and slid a book across the table: *A Primer of Chess* by Jose Capablanca.

Ali smiled and held out two shackled fists to Walker, palms down. Walker pointed to the left one. Ali's fingers unfurled like a sea anemone, his long fingers fluttering to reveal one of the white pawn replicas resting on his now flat palm. The second fist rolled open: a black pawn. The ritual meant Walker would have the white pieces, and the all-important first move. Ali leaned forward, and an army of chess men fashioned from stale bread cascaded onto the table from beneath his shirt; a small red and white checked tablecloth followed. Walker smiled and began to set up the pieces.

To his surprise, he found himself more or less holding his own; well into the mid game, he was down only one bishop and a single pawn to the younger player. Somewhere toward the end of the first hour, however, the checkered grid became a clogged and cluttered wasteland, a battlefield without pattern or possibility. Walker watched helplessly as Ali's black army sliced through his depleted forces, moving as if on iron rails, forcefully and with purpose. Walker's captured pieces now sat in a neat row in front of Ali, milky white against the blood red of his prison jumpsuit.

Walker tipped over his queen and pushed back his chair.

"It was not quite hopeless, you know," Ali smiled. "You gave up too soon."

"Story of my life," Walker responded, pinching the bridge of his nose and shaking the cobwebs from his head.

As Ali set up the pieces for another game, Walker began to sift through his reporter's notebook. His morning canvass of downtown optometrists had been something of a bust: no one could identify Allan Singleton's picture and the name Ollie Drupt rang no bells. A call to Public Works about permits to convert bank vaults into human residences yielded a chuckle from the clerk who answered the phone, but no hard information. Maybe David Singleton was wrong—perhaps his brother didn't want to be found after all.

Walker continued to flip through his scrawled notes. Most were shorthand reminders to himself, elliptical and coded. Often a page dealing with one assignment would inexplicably run into notes from other cases. The disorder was in part by design. Walker knew that were he ever required to turn over his notes in court, the opposing side would need either a cryptologist or an archeologist to decipher them. So far, though, nothing in the notes pointed to the whereabouts of Allan Singleton.

Walker levered his eyes away from the notebook and back to Ali. "Tell me about her. About Noor."

Ali's slender fingers worked to reshape a bent "rook" before placing it on its proper square. For a moment, the muscles in his jaw stood out like ropes. "You wouldn't understand," he said, exhaling a long sigh.

Walker closed his notebook. "Maybe I would. Try me."

"She disgraced the family."

"Benjamin Navarro?"

"She was his whore," Ali whispered.

"That's a pretty heavy judgment, Ali."

"I knew you wouldn't understand."

"Your father tells me you were very close to her."

"Of course I was," Ali replied, defiance creeping into his voice. "We talked about what we would do when we grew up, about how she wanted to study microbiology in college. We encouraged and supported each other's dreams."

"And your father?"

"He wanted the best for her, too…"

The voice softer now, Walker noted.

"What happened to those dreams?"

"Benjamin happened. His big car happened, and the gold chains around his neck happened." Ali convulsively crushed the rook in his hand before continuing. "My father said he represented everything that is wrong with America. But Noor went out with him every night. Her back was turned on the family. So my father said we should shun her and treat her like the whore she had become and stop talking to her."

"Did you stop talking to her?"

Ali nodded.

"Did you think she was a whore?"

Ali looked down at his manacled wrists. Walker leaned forward and took the crumpled chess piece from his fingers.

"Is that why you shot her?" Walker asked quietly.

Ali's chest heaved with a great intake of air. After a moment, his eyes found Walker's face. "I didn't...there was no other choice."

Ali's shoulders rose in sudden, great sobs. Walker left his chair and went around the table. He placed his arm around the boy's heaving shoulders and knelt next to him. Ali's head dropped to his chest. Walker's hand squeezed the boy's bony shoulder.

After what seemed like a long time, Ali's breathing slowed and the sobbing stopped. Walker stared hard into the middle distance, a small pulse working in his jaw.

CHAPTER SIX

Walker left the jail and went around the corner to the Hall of Justice. With a quick show of his laminated license, he bypassed the metal detector and entered the main lobby. He purchased a pack of gum from the blind candy vendor. As he waited impatiently for an elevator, his eyes reflexively skimmed the small dramas and shadow plays unfolding on benches and outside closed court room doors: cops and D.A.s rehearsing testimony to be delivered in court in the next few minutes; a few lawyers huddled with clients while others worked their cell phones, oblivious to the foot traffic eddying and swirling around them, stood rooted to the floor, their heads tilted like trees in a high wind.

Walker nodded absently to Dan Bertini, a high-profile P.I. to the rich and famous, resplendent in his two thousand dollar Armani suit whose broad checkered pattern called to mind a carnival barker. In a far corner, Walker saw the distinctive gray ponytail of a noted criminal defense attorney known for his Halloween parties attended by judges, poets, hookers and his dope dealer clients. The lawyer was deep in conversation with a short-haired man conservatively dressed in a business suit. *Must be a client*, Walker thought.

The elevator arrived and dropped Walker to the basement. The doors closed behind him and Walker advanced towards a floor to ceiling wire cage at the end of the hall. The air was thick, almost palpable. Walker rang a small bell that seemed more suitable to a motel desk. Moments passed, and a thirtyish uniformed officer with a sour expression appeared. Walker guessed he was a member of the Bow and Arrow Squad—cops, who for reasons of alleged or real misconduct, had been stripped of their guns and reassigned to clerical duties.

Walker explained who he was and what he wanted. The clerk disappeared and several long moments passed. Walker guessed that a call went upstairs to the Homicide Unit to confirm that he was indeed who he claimed to be. He pulled out his notebook and began to leaf through his Singleton notes. A scribbled postcard from Allan he had not yet read caught Walker's attention. In it, Allan described his new optometrist's office as located "near the Egyptian Consulate." *Bingo,* Walker thought. *I got you now, you little fucker.* A smile broke across his face.

The clerk reappeared, glanced quizzically at Walker, and handed him a disappointingly slim Manila envelope. Walker put away his notebook and opened the envelope. He quickly scanned a single-page lab report, which confirmed that test firings from the gun Hassan Bakkrat had turned over to the police displayed the same land and groove markings as the lead slugs found in Noor Bakkrat's body. No surprises there, Walker realized.

A second sheet of paper summarized a test for gunpowder residue on Ali's hands. The results were consistent with chemicals normally found after the discharge of a firearm. Walker knew that this test was not always conclusive, that it often generated false positive results. For example, roofers and construction workers used chemicals that could give the same test results. Walker speculated that Benjamin Navarro, Noor's automobile-body painter-boy friend, could have fired the gun and no test could ever convict him. Yet no one doubted that Ali was the shooter. But where did he get the gun?

Walker asked the clerk for the weapon. The original description in the police report had been quite sketchy and he needed to see the actual gun. It proved to be an inexpensive 9mm automatic, silver in color, unremarkable, ordinary even, but quite lethal. Walker knew that in this or any other large city, this gun could be acquired on the street within an hour by almost anyone. Still, Walker wondered how a Palestinian teenager like Ali, so lacking in street smarts, could come by such a weapon. The low-life boy friend, however, certainly would know where to get one. What if he provided the gun, gave it to Ali? Well, that didn't make sense—why would a sensitive, intelligent young man kill the sister he clearly loved?

Nothing about this made sense, Walker told himself, and handed the gun and the envelope back to the clerk. For a case that appeared open and shut, there were too many unanswered questions. He looked at his watch: there would be time before meeting Linda to check out the Egyptian Consulate.

City Vision Optometrists was located on Clay Street off Montgomery, which placed the store in the Financial District, technically just beyond downtown and Walker's initial canvass of eyeglass stores. It was a small shop dating from perhaps the 1920's, with a checkered tile floor and high ceilings. A large pair of glasses made from neon tubing perched jauntily above the doorway. Walker left the MG at a nearby parking meter, which he covered with a paper bag. He knew this ruse seldom worked, but one had to resort to desperate measures in a city with something like 3.1 cars per parking place.

Before entering the shop, Walker looked up at the pyramid-shaped Transamerica world headquarters looming overhead a block away. During one of his previous incarnations, Walker had driven cab for a few months, and one of the first things he'd learned from veteran drivers was the appropriate response to inevitable queries from out of town visitors about this distinctive building. Unsuspecting tourists were cheerfully informed that the building was the Egyptian Consulate. It was, of course, no such thing. The real consulate was several miles away in Pacific Heights, a high-priced residential district with no nearby coffee shops.

Five minutes later, Walker emerged from City Vision, ʾed the paper bag from the meter, and fired up the MG. ʾ blocks and three turns later, he was on the ʾero, heading north along the renovated waterfront. A young female assistant had easily recognized Allan Singleton's picture. After some initial skepticism, she listened with interest to Walker's request for an address, made with all the charm and grace he could deliver on behalf of a representative of a family member looking for a lost relative. She went to the back of the shop to confer with an older man, who sized Walker up from a distance, and returned moments later with something in her hand. "My uncle was in the Korean War," she smiled at Walker. "His best friend suffered shell shock and forgot his own name." She handed Walker a piece of paper with an address for Ollie Drupt at the base of Telegraph Hill.

Weaving in and out of a jagged slalom course of orange traffic cones, Walker edged the speedometer needle ten miles over the limit as he sped along the Embarcadero. Once home to the cargo ships serviced by Harry Bridges' proud longshoremen and the great Matson ocean liners that carried passengers to Hawaii, abandoned and derelict piers sullenly awaited their inevitable conversion into architect's offices or upscale restaurants. It seemed to Walker that everywhere he went the city was changing, mindlessly consuming its past and lurching toward a brave new future he was not at all sure he liked.

Walker left the waterfront and found parking next to a 24-hour exercise club. He made his way on foot past the Filbert Steps, the steep incline that lead to the top of Telegraph Hill and Walker's neighborhood. For a fleeting moment, the repertory movie theatre housed in the back of Walker's head came to life and brought up an image of Humphrey Bogart playing the part of a man falsely accused of murder in the film *Dark Passage*, trudging up and down these same stairs. At least Bogart had Lauren Bacall and her Art Deco apartment waiting for him at the top as a reward. The real-life apartment was around the corner from Walker's, where, Walker reminded himself, not often enough Linda—but always Archie—waited for him.

A squat, concrete housing complex for senior citizens nestled amidst converted warehouses and yet another athletic club. Walker checked the address; it was indeed the one Ollie Drupt had given City Vision. He entered through sliding double glass doors and walked past several men and women in a day room, placidly watching television from marooned wheel chairs. Walker found the office and went in.

A lanky, pleasant-featured forty-something woman with deep, velvety brown eyes and dark pageboy bangs worked the phone and talked simultaneously with a female resident with powdery blue hair and an older man dressed in neatly pressed work clothes. The man's sun-leathered skin and gnarled hands suggested years of physical work: *the building maintenance man,* Walker thought as he seated himself in a chair to wait for the woman to conclude her juggling act and acknowledge his presence. The woman whose nametag read Juliana Broderick smiled at Walker and continued talking. The smile was truly dazzling. Walker slid Allan's photograph along with his business card across the table. She looked down, nodded vigorously, held up a finger, and mouthed silently: "One minute." Walker nodded back.

Five minutes later, Juliana Broderick hung up the phone.

"The shuttle bus will be here at a quarter to, Mrs. Levinson," she told the woman with the blue rinse, who muttered something to herself and left the room.

Broderick turned to Walker.

"We wondered when you'd come."

"I'm not sure I know what you mean," Walker responded, retrieving the photograph.

"Ollie was our mystery boarder, wasn't he, Harry?"

"Sure as hell was." Harry's hands came to life and for a moment fluttered like small birds before subsiding in his lap. "Thought he might have been a Nazi war criminal or one of those terrorist types. He sure was one strange fellow."

Broderick shook her head, a frown appearing on her smooth forehead.

"Not all of us went quite that far. But we did have ˙tions. There was nothing in his file, no family history, no ˙ound. He just showed up one day."

"How did he qualify to be in a senior center?" Walker ˙ wasn't even sixty."

"We have several open slots for social service clients. He arrived with all the right paperwork," Broderick replied. "Five years ago, when the building opened, it was one of the conditions attached to our mandate that we reserve a few slots for the general population."

"Can you tell me what the building was used for before you folks took over?"

"I've only been here eighteen months." Broderick turned to Harry. "You must know, Harry."

"A warehouse for the Bank of Commerce," Harry replied, absently scratching what looked like a liver spot on the back of one hand. "It was a warehouse. They stored all their punch cards and cancelled checks here. Before computers, you know. Gave it to the city and got a big tax write off."

"Might I ask why you're looking for him, Mr....?" Broderick's brown eyes bore down on Walker now.

"Walker, Ms. Broderick. I was hired by his brother to find him."

"Has he done anything wrong?"

"We don't believe so. His brother is concerned for him; he's been out of touch."

"Unfortunately, you're too late." She checked a list on her desk. "He moved out last Thursday. Left no forwarding address."

"Would it be possible for me to see his room?"

Broderick looked at Harry and then back at Walker.

"I don't see why not. The room is not protected by any confidentiality issues. *He* would have been, you know. We wouldn't have even been able to tell you if he were a resident when he was here."

"I understand."

Broderick's smile filled the room for a moment and then was gone.

Harry rose from his seat. "I can take him up, Miss Juliana."

"Thank you, Harry." She returned to her desk. Walker wondered how many times a day the smile was allowed to escape.

Walker followed Harry, trying not to run up the slower man's back as he shuffled down a long corridor. Harry paused before a door two-thirds of the way down the hall, and laboriously sorted through a jangling ring of keys. Walker looked up and down the corridor. Muted sounds of television programs leaked from under doors, laughter rising and falling mechanically. Afternoon talk shows, Walker thought. Harry opened the door and stood back.

Walker entered a room that could have doubled as a London blitz air-raid shelter: cracked and fissured walls painted black, every window covered with dark blue construction paper. Harry mumbled something and began to tear off the covering and open windows.

"They know they can't decorate their rooms on their own," Harry mumbled. "But they still go ahead and do it." He half-heartedly tore some of the paper from the windows. Weak light seeped into the room.

Walker flipped the wall switch and a single overhead lamp drove most of the shadows back into the edges of the room. A narrow daybed stood in a corner near a battered wooden dresser. Near the door, there was a cramped kitchen area consisting of a rusted sink and small refrigerator.

Walker began with the kitchen. Carefully washed empty tin cans stood in a neat line on the washboard. The labels read peas, succotash, tuna fish. Walker opened a drawer: clean silverware and some utensils.

Harry leaned in and started counting. "Yep, all there," he said brightly. "We supply the gear; they get their own grub if they want."

Walker drifted over to a thrift store wooden desk and chair. He ran his hand across the flaking top. The central drawer was empty, save for a well-chewed pencil, a few loose postage stamps in denominations at least a year out of date, and a well-thumbed paperback claiming to contain a mathematical system "to make millions at black jack."

Walker approached the dresser and methodically slid the drawers out and turned them over. He lifted the mattress and peered at the bed springs. Nothing.

Walker moved to the center of the room. He scanned the bare walls. No paintings, no pictures, no human touch. Moving closer, he noticed a bare rectangular patch of wall with a lighter shade of paint. At least he had one painting, Walker told himself. He leaned closer. At the center of the rectangle, four small pieces of cellophane tape formed the points of a perfect five-inch square. Something small and flat had been taped there. Something the size of a computer compact disc, Walker thought. Walker turned toward the door, thanked Harry and walked out of the room.

Walker passed Juliana's office. The phone was once more braced between her neck and shoulder, her body leaning into the conversation, one long leg bent under her, the other straight out. He wondered what it would be like to have dinner with Juliana Broderick, away from this depressing building and the rules and strictures of her life. Worried that these thoughts would brand him as unfaithful to Linda, Walker told himself that fantasies alone did not count.

Walker pointed the sports car toward the Embarcadero and home. Moving with the late afternoon commuter traffic and directly into the setting sun, he adjusted his rearview mirror and for a moment he thought he saw, two cars behind him, the familiar brown van from last week's parking confrontation. Before he could be certain, a delivery truck blocked his view. Walker felt his insides tighten. He decided he might want to dig out the .38 Detective Special from the closet when he got home.

CHAPTER SEVEN

Walker deftly speared a pork-filled dumpling swimming in a light film of soy sauce on his plate. His appreciation and understanding of chopsticks was recent. Not the use of them—he had always been a more or less credible stick man at countless dinners at Chinese restaurants on both coasts—but the cosmic significance of the tapered wooden shafts had eluded him until Linda explained that cold and metal are enemies of health for the Chinese.

"Metal is cold, and is not used with food," she explained. "That's why you see the old men in Portsmouth Square drinking hot water in the morning."

Walker wondered why some of these same old men smoked liked chimneys if they were so health-minded.

"Balance, Walker," Linda replied sweetly. Walker, not buying, nodded.

The conversation was taking place in the upstairs fluorescent-lit, linoleum-floored dining room of Sam Woo's, a hole-in-the-wall restaurant legendary for waiters who disdained writing down orders and where bills were reckoned by inventorying leftover plates. Linda murmured a few words in Cantonese to an elderly waiter, who reappeared moments later with a large tureen of hot and sour fish soup not listed on the menu. Walker, taking note of bits of mushroom and unknown maritime life floating on the surface, hesitatingly brought a spoonful to his mouth. His eyes burned with tears. The sensation was not entirely unpleasant and the soup tasted surprisingly good.

During Linda's early childhood, her engineer father often spent months abroad building dams and airports for third world potentates. After her mother's death during childbirth, much of Linda's upbringing reverted by default to an Asian housekeeper, a recent immigrant from Hong Kong who spoke no English. As a result, Linda could speak Cantonese more or less fluently. Reading it, however, was another matter. The downside of this rather exotic upbringing was an often solitary and isolated childhood. "I don't play well with others," Linda warned him the first week they met.

The meal continued with Linda ordering off-menu dishes for them to sample. Finally, his eyes glazed and belly full, Walker fingered a fortune cookie and cracked it open.

"'You will be remembered for your good deeds'" he read. "True, but boring."

Linda opened hers.

"'You bring excitement and pleasure to your friends.' Well, I do my best."

"Generic platitudes," Walker replied, stretching his arms above his head and yawning.

"You can make them more interesting."

"How?"

"Just add 'in bed' after each sentence."

"I will be remembered for my good deeds...in bed?"

"As I bring excitement and pleasure."

"Not bad, Linda."

"Thank you, Walker."

Walker slowly brought his arms down. His spine felt tense, flexed and loaded.

"It's been a long day. Let's go home."

"We need to talk," Linda answered, rooted to her chair.

"About?"

"About us."

"What about us?"

"All we do is eat and have sex."

"What's wrong with that?"

"Nothing. Everything." Linda's fingered the shards of what remained of her fortune cookie. "It's not enough, Walker. At least for me, it isn't."

"When these two cases wind down, maybe we can get away to Mendocino for a long weekend," Walker said quietly.

"It isn't that. We never talk."

"That's plain fucking not true." His voice ratcheted up several notches and quickly fell back. "We talk all the time."

Linda pushed away her plate and looked around. Several customers seemed interested in their conversation. She lowered her voice and leaned across the table, her face inches from Walker's.

"When you talk about anything other than work, your eyes glaze over," Linda whispered. "You treat anything that doesn't have to do with one of your cases as an interlude, as if you're waiting for the main event to come back on stage."

Wanting to defend himself, Walker forced himself to listen.

"You're obsessive and obsessed," Linda continued. "And I understand it perfectly. I know it comes with the job. I even respect that. But it doesn't make for a very flowing relationship."

"Linda," Walker began. He paused, and started again. "When we're together, I am very much with you. You know that."

Linda's fingers covered the back of Walker's hand, her eyes seeming to search for something in his face.

After a moment, he felt the light pressure of her fingers recede.

"It's been a long day," he said quietly. "Let's go home."

They got up and Walker tossed some bills on the table.

The morning sun sliced through the Venetian blinds like a hot knife, raking the bed with long zebra-striped shadows. Walker, flat on his stomach, opened one eye and read the clock: 7:20. His bare right arm reached out across the bed to emptiness. Twisting his head to look, he saw that Linda was gone. He rose, dressed, and made his version of campfire coffee and took the steaming cup to the window. He stared out at the bay for several long minutes.

Three-quarters of an hour later, Walker stood on the steps of the Hall of Justice waiting for Malcolm Delucca to come out of court. Attorneys and cops who had escaped the building to grab a cigarette clustered under a thin blue haze of cigarette smoke. Walker deposited quarters into a vending machine and retrieved a copy of the *San Francisco Chronicle,* discarding into a trashcan everything except the local news and sports. An article on Harrison Bledsoe caught his eye. The local philanthropist Allan Singleton had ranted against was scheduled to speak the following week at an outdoor gathering on the Embarcadero. If anyone wanted to harm Bledsoe, this was a serious window of opportunity. Walker told himself he needed to crank up his efforts to find Singleton.

Delucca, red suspenders smoldering beneath his dark blue "courtroom" suit, strode out of the building and up to Walker. The attorney's face looked tired, strained.

"I just came from Department Twenty-One," Delucca said, lighting a cigarette. "The judge will rule by the end of the week whether Ali can be tried as an adult."

He dragged heavily on the cigarette.

"He's still a kid," Walker responded.

Delucca took another long drag, looked at the cigarette as if it were a strange object, and dropped it to the pavement.

"Doesn't matter. Look at the times, Walker."

Delucca ground the cigarette under his heel. "Got anything for me?"

"Yes and no."

"That's great, Walker. Hell, if you don't have anything, you could at least pretend that you did."

"You want me to lie, Malcolm?"

"Remember Henry Hathaway?"

Walker nodded. An image floated up of an earnest, plodding investigator now on the fringe of the business.

"I hired him to do a simple tail job last year. He lost the guy at a traffic light. Blew the entire surveillance. Of course, I fired him."

Walker, uncomfortable now, wondered where this was going.

"That happens. Tail jobs only work perfectly in movies, Counselor."

"That's not why I fired him. I canned his ass because he was too dumb to lie. He couldn't even make up a story about the subject suddenly cranking his car up to ninety on the freeway. Something—anything—would have been better than what he told me."

Walker wondered if Delucca had just handed him an encrypted message, a veiled suggestion that Walker's own marketability as an investigator might be enhanced if clients thought he was not above the occasional and judicious piece of deception. He knew certain investigators cultivated that kind of gray reputation. True or not, the perception wasn't bad for business. For a moment, Walker worried that he might be on the downward slope of a career if an old client like Delucca had to drop this kind of hint. Or was the immediate defensiveness he felt at the lawyer's remarks in the end simply his own paranoia, first triggered by the gentle early morning earthquake earlier in the week, now full blown?

"What I can tell you is there're some pieces that don't fit. The gun, for instance…how Ali came by it in the first place. His motive, for another, since he doesn't seem to be a religious fanatic."

"That's what I'm paying you for. To find this stuff out."

"I know. I just want to make sure you understand that there're a lot of loose threads here. You pull on one and something you don't like might be on the other end."

"I understand. Just keep me informed." Delucca glanced down at the mashed cigarette. "How the hell did you quit—the patch?"

"Watching TV over one long Labor Day weekend did it for me."

Delucca reached out and squeezed Walker's shoulder, smiled, and turned to move down the steps when he saw Benjamin Navarro push through the front door, his face mottled and clouded.

"He's been in court every day," Delucca whispered to Walker. "Today at recess, he let out a yell and took two steps toward Ali until the bailiff stopped him with his baton. The guy's scary."

Delucca flashed a quick smile and descended the steps to the sidewalk.

Walker watched Navarro turn left and head down Bryant toward Sixth Street, apparently headed toward the wholesale flower market. The Latino mechanic moved with the rolling gait of a sailor on shore leave and Walker had to hurry to keep up. Navarro entered a café favored by a mix of lawyers, cops, loading-dock workers, and flower cutters. By the time Walker got to the entrance, Navarro was seated at the counter, coffee steaming in a chipped green mug beside his elbow.

Walker settled into the next seat and studied the menu. Navarro glanced at Walker, turned his shoulder away, and hunched over his coffee.

Walker ordered a Caesar salad and a glass of iced tea.

"Look, I told you I'm not interested in talking to anyone who works for Ali Bakkrat." The words left Navarro's mouth like metal shavings falling to the floor.

"I understand."

Walker's ice tea arrived. He tore the top off a packet of sugar substitute and poured half the contents into his glass.

"Jesus."

"Jesus what?" Navarro said, his head half-cocked toward Walker.

Walker held up the packet.

"Check this out…'known to cause cancer in laboratory animals.' The things we do to keep the pounds off."

Navarro didn't say anything.

"I'm a walking contradiction …" Walker continued.

"You want to know something?" Navarro asked evenly. "I don't give a fuck what you are."

A waitress refilled Navarro's mug. Walker's salad arrived and he launched into it.

"I'm trying to get my head around this case," Walker began, his words muffled by the Romaine lettuce in his mouth. "A lot of it just doesn't make sense."

Navarro shook his head from side to side.

"You don't get it, do you?"

Walker raised his shoulders in an inquiring shrug.

"It's not supposed to make sense," Navarro went on, his voice rising. "The whole fucking family is extremists from the fucking stone age. Nothing they do is normal."

Navarro turned on his stool so he faced Walker.

"They did every fucking thing to keep us apart, man. They lectured her, tried to ground her, they even brought in some mullah person from South City to talk to her."

"How did she react?"

"Lots of nights she couldn't sleep." Navarro ran his index finger around the lip of his coffee cup. "She would wake up and cling to me."

Navarro's voice faltered and broke.

"You want to know the truth?" His eyes were bright and shiny. "The truth was she loved me and I loved her."

Walker pushed his salad away and watched a flood of emotion march across Navarro's face as he raked the back of a fist across his cheekbones.

"Sounds like they came at her from all sides. Who was the heavy in this, who pushed the most?"

"I wondered the same thing. When I asked Noor, she would just shut down and clam up."

Navarro took a long sip from his coffee cup. Walker waited for him to continue.

"I was raised on a truck farm outside of Visalia," Navarro said, his voice filled with self-mocking bitterness. "My old man thought whipping the shit out of me and my brother was how you raised a kid. Naturally, I ran away as soon as I fucking could. I got in my share of trouble, did time in the joint, all that." He paused, unconsciously rubbing the tattoo on his forearm. "But the beautiful thing about Noor, she accepted me for who I was. I guess she knew what it was like to be an outsider. Sometimes I think we must've come from the same egg basket. Now that little punk took her away from me."

"Ali doesn't come across as someone who would murder his sister."

"Bullshit. He's a stone-cold killer." Navarro pushed his coffee cup away. "Open your eyes, man."

Navarro put a crumpled dollar on the counter and was gone.

Walker retrieved his car and drove north on Sixth Street. After several blocks, he crossed an invisible border into what detectives and cab drivers called the Wine Country, an area of blight and human despair dotted with liquor stores, transient hotels, and peep show arcades. A few brave souls—mostly working artists and other free spirits—had found refuge and cheap housing in the neighborhood and were beginning to make their presence known. Walker passed a vacant building that had been transformed into something called the "Defenestration Hotel" and smiled as he saw the bathtubs, chairs, and standing lamps poking and protruding at crazy angles from the building's façade. He wished he could meet the anonymous pranksters to thank them for this free-spirited assault on what people liked to think of as "public art."

He had no trouble parking on the street. Meters rose from the cracked and sloping concrete sidewalk and a half dozen empty spaces vied for his attention. Walker pulled into one and fed the meter with as many quarters as it would take. Reflexively, he looked up and down the street: no brown van. Walker wove his way through a human picket fence of panhandlers, crackheads and the lost and broken, until he came to an address in the middle of the block.

The store was so out of place it seemed to pulsate. Lettering on the spotless plate glass window announced MIDDLE EASTERN IMPORTED FOODS. Inside Walker saw clusters of hanging garlic, bags of what looked like Basmati rice, and earthen bowls containing multi-colored powders. He entered, setting off a soft tinkling of bells above the door. The scent of the store was overwhelming, sensual.

A fiftyish man with a neatly-stubbled beard and sharp, dark eyes appeared from the rear of the store. He wore a pressed blue apron over a charcoal gray sweater and tan slacks.

"Yes? May I help you?"

"I hope you can."

"We don't get many walk-in customers...most of our business is for restaurants." The voice was even, pleasant. "My name is Mohammed Bakkrat, I own this store."

Walker handed him his business card. "Your brother, Hassan, hired me, Mr. Bakkrat. I am working on your nephew's case."

"I see." Bakkrat looked at the face of the card and turned it over, carefully examining the back as if it contained a hidden message. "It is a very sad time for our family."

"Yes, I understand."

"How can I be of assistance?"

Looking for a place to sit, Walker began to move toward a large wooden barrel.

"Please. Join for me coffee," Bakkrat intervened, gesturing toward an airless cubicle swimming in dust motes illuminated by a single overhead skylight.

The men sat inches apart, facing each other, their knees almost touching.   Moments later, Walker found himself balancing a small demitasse of very strong coffee on one knee. He noticed a dusty chess set resting on a nearby packing crate.

"Do you play chess, Mr. Bakkrat?"

"Oh, no. That belongs to Ali. He uses it to practice when he visits."

"I see."

Neither man spoke for several moments.

"This is an indescribable tragedy," Bakkrat began. "Noor was a very beautiful child. My brother was very close to her. He adopted Noor when our third brother, Ahmed, was killed in the first *Intifada.*

"I was not aware of that."

"You know the *Intifada*, Mr. Walker?" Bakkrat asked, his eyes unwaveringly on Walker now.

"Yes. It was the uprising in the occupied territories in Israel."

"In Palestine, Mr. Walker."

"Yes. Please continue, Mr. Bakkrat."

Bakkrat poured more coffee into Walker's cup. Walker's insides churned as he watched the thick grounds swirl and settle.

"My brother was very protective of Noor," Bakkrat continued. "Perhaps because of the guilt he felt."

"Please explain."

"You see, our brother Ahmed was very active in the resistance. Hassan was a religious man, and did not participate in militant organizations. When Ahmed was killed by an Israeli mortar shell, Hassan was devastated. He told me he must pay for his inactivity by adopting his niece. He felt he had to protect her from the bad things the world could bring down on a person. As a result, he kept her away from people and spent a lot of time with her himself."

"Please continue." Walker placed his cup on the floor.

"When the family came to the United States, the children saw America as a candy store. A wonderful candy store. Hassan tried to hold to the old ways, to Muslim tenets and beliefs, but Noor in particular had no interest in formal religion. When she started going with that boy—the garage mechanic—it was the last straw. In our culture, Mr. Walker, for a young woman to offer her virginity to the first person she meets is more than a sin, it is a tragedy."

"Is that how Ali saw it?"

"You must understand, Mr. Walker, my observations are just speculations," Bakkrat replied with a wan smile. "I was not around his family all the time. I have this business and my own family. But I can imagine that it must have been devastating for Ali when he saw the wonderful girl he had grown up with as a sister change utterly and completely before his eyes. And as for killing her, I can only say that is not the Muslim way. It is true that in some Islamic countries women who behave in the manner Noor did would be ostracized, perhaps even stoned in public. But not killed, Mr. Walker."

"Then what Ali did was an aberration?"

"In terms of our culture and our people, yes."

"If I understand you correctly, Mr. Bakkrat, you are saying that Ali's act had both a moral and a personal component."

"It is really much more an American trait...to solve matters through violence." Bakkrat picked up Walker's cup and carried it to a small sink in the corner. "I understand that most murders in this country are committed by family members," he said, rinsing the cup under the faucet.

"Or someone known to the victim," Walker added.

"Yes, of course. As human beings, we have many dimensions."

"Did Ali ever show any interest in guns?"

"Not that I know of, Mr. Walker. Since Ahmed died resisting Israeli oppression, no one in this family is particularly fond of guns."

Bakkrat's face had drawn tight and closed. He turned back from the sink and his lips creased into a thin smile as he placed the now dry cup on a shelf above the sink.

"Mr. Walker, I must return to work. I have many customers whose orders I need to fill. I hope you understand."

Walker rose and moved toward the door. When he looked back, Bakkrat was already seated at a computer screen.

"One more question, Mr. Bakkrat."

"Yes?" Bakkrat's head swiveled toward Walker.

"Do you happen to own a gun?"

"Yes, I do...for the store only. As you can see, we are not in the safest neighborhood."

"May I ask what kind?"

"I believe it is an automatic. A nine-millimeter. But I am no expert in guns."

"If it would not be too much trouble, might I take a look at it?"

Bakkrat's shoulders rose in a shrug.

"Three weekends ago I discovered it was missing."

"Was anything else taken?"

"No," Bakkrat replied. He gestured vaguely toward the rear of the store. "Some of the windows are old and not secure. It is easy to break in."

"Did you report the theft?"

"To the insurance company, yes. To the police, no."

"Why not?"

"Nothing else was taken. There was no need to involve the police."

Walker, who had involuntarily drawn in his breath, felt himself exhale slowly.

"You think it is the gun Ali used, don't you?" Bakkrat's eyes were sharp and focused.

"I can't say, Mr. Bakkrat," Walker heard himself respond.

Walker took a few steps toward the door and then turned back.

"I think it would be best that you not mention the gun to anyone just yet. At least until I speak with Ali's attorney."

Bakkrat held his gaze and nodded slowly. Walker pushed through the door and into the bright light. His eyes narrowed as he walked quickly to his car.

CHAPTER EIGHT

Walker put off reporting his findings to Delucca and instead spent the following morning on the phone tracking down former faculty colleagues of Allan Singleton. Not surprisingly, Walker discovered that university professors, like their counterparts in other large corporate entities, were shielded from the intrusions of the outside world by an elaborate phone mail system. By noon, only one person had directly responded. Toby Wolfson, an associate professor of mathematics, generously agreed to see Walker later that afternoon in his Berkeley office. Although Walker told him little about the nature of his visit, Wolfson volunteered that he had always liked Singleton, but was not surprised that the "little fucker" was in trouble.

Now, as he drove across the Bay Bridge in light traffic, the brisk offshore breeze thumping and rattling the MG's canvas top, Walker located his cell phone under his seat, punched a code, and wedged the phone in the visor in front of him. As he gave Delucca a concise summary of his conversation with Mohammed Bakkrat, Walker watched the afternoon sun playing tag with the huge cranes on the Oakland docks.

"Planning and premeditation, just what we needed..." Delucca's voice was thin but clear.

"I know," Walker responded.

"Are we sure Ali had access to the store?"

"According to the uncle, yes. He even kept a chess set there."

"Shit."

"Yes."

"So where the hell are we now?" Delucca demanded.

"We can assume if I found out about the gun, the police will too. At least by the time of trial."

"Right. Maybe we should try to keep this Bakkrat uncle out of the spotlight for a while."

"What do you want me to do—tell him to go to Disneyland?"

"Christ, Walker. This is serious."

"I am being serious."

"At least you didn't find the actual gun. Then we would be sitting on the horns of another dilemma."

"The cops have the gun, Malcolm."

"I know, I know." Walker thought he heard the crackle of cellophane—Delucca going for a new pack. "But according to the canon of legal ethics, a lawyer or his agent—you being the agent here, Walker—must turn over to the prosecution any physical evidence he or she discovers suggesting that a crime has or will be committed."

"Hell, I know that, Malcolm," Walker responded, fighting to keep irritation out of his voice. "In this case, I didn't find anything. I repeat, I found *nothing*. But I'll be damned if I'll do the prosecution's work by telling them how our client happened to come by the weapon that was used in a homicide."

"Certainly not." Delucca paused and Walker imagined the lawyer dragging on his cigarette. "But in that little hypothetical of mine, one of us could lose his license. It's not worth it, Walker."

"No, it isn't," Walker answered, feeling his insides tighten. Walker wondered if Delucca saw him as someone who had trouble playing by the rules of the game and was using this hypothetical as a warning to him. In the same moment, he realized in his own moral universe, there could conceivably come a time when he would walk away from his profession over the kind of issue Delucca had raised.   Walker chose not share this thought with the attorney.

There was a pause, both men backing off.

"You're not stalling me, are you, Walker?"

"Me? Never, Malcolm." Walker hoped the other man could hear the smile in his voice.

"I think I got a good chance of getting bail for Ali next week."

"Great."

The little car edged past the east footing of the bridge. Walker needed to merge across three lanes of traffic to get to the freeway he wanted.

"I gotta go, Malcolm. To be continued."

"To be continued." Delucca's voice was tense and tired as he cut the connection.

Walker removed the phone from the visor and stowed it under his seat. He realized that Delucca was right to worry about the seemingly rudderless investigation. On the other hand, Walker felt, in ways he found difficult to articulate to someone else, let alone himself, that often his best work grew from time spent in seeming stasis, in mulling and sifting and following dead-end leads. He sensed that somewhere in his recent conversation with Ali's uncle small fragments of the puzzle were beginning to come unstuck. Tiny seismic shifts were occurring. The larger pieces, however, stubbornly refused to give up their meaning.

Walker approached the campus from its soft southern underbelly. In the late 60's, the university attempted to erect a *cordon sanitaire* in the area—what had been a large, open air "people's park" was fenced in and a faceless dormitory was scheduled to go up until massive street demonstrations and the spectacle of the National Guard marching through the center of the city with fixed bayonets thwarted this plan.   Telegraph Avenue, the major point of entry to the campus, now awash in new shops and restaurants, still retained its inherently rebellious character: artisans sat at tables displaying their wares as young arrivals from America's suburbs continued to gather on street corners, smoking various aromatic substances and playing musical instruments.

Walker parked several blocks away. He remembered arriving a quarter of a century ago, a wide-eyed immigrant from the east coast, fearlessly venturing into Berkeley like some expectant cosmonaut. Now, he felt more like the Ancient Mariner.

A block ahead, the gate to one of the world's pre-eminent institutions opened to take him in. The entrance defined the border between two worlds—one devoted to the life of the mind and the other to the unruly life of the street. Both seemed to Walker to complement each other, existing as two halves of the same whole. He thought of Linda and her use of the word "balance." He pinched his nose, worried that he was becoming soft-headed in his slide into advanced middle age.

The graduate mathematics office was located in a leafy quadrangle off the main campus. A somber, slate-gray façade was split by several Doric columns wound with gnarled tendrils of, what appeared to be, a venerable wisteria vine climbed skyward. A uniformed campus police officer stopped Walker to ask for ID. Walker wondered if this heightened state of alertness was the legacy of Ted Kaczynski, who three decades earlier had been a promising young faculty member in this very department until madness and alienation drove him to become the feared Unabomber. Walker resolved to ask Toby Wolfson what it was about the advanced study of mathematics that made people crazy. He showed the guard his laminated P.I. license and was directed to the professor's office.

The door was ajar, and Walker heard what he took to be a basketball broadcast. Peering in, he saw a man his age with his feet up on a polished oak desk in front of a portable TV the size of a small cereal box. Wolfson was watching a playoff basketball game on the tiny screen, the players small as mice. Squinting, Walker saw two storied and revered Phoenix Suns execute a perfect pick and roll. The former player still alive within Walker savored the moment.

Wolfson gestured for him to enter. Walker came in and looked around. The office was spare and lean, in contrast to the man who sat across the desk. Walker guessed that Wolfson, who appeared to be barely five feet six inches tall, weighed in at least two hundred and forty pounds. A face like a pale moon floated above a loose plaid shirt and baggy cargo pants with pockets on the outside. The overall effect was almost cherubic.

Walker searched in vain for a blackboard where he expected to see equations scribbled in chalk. Instead, one wall was covered with a Grateful Dead poster, on the other a cork bulletin board boasted pictures of Wilt Chamberlain, Alfred Hitchcock and Sophia Loren. Walker and Wolfson sat silently for a good minute, unable to take their eyes from the postage-stamp screen.

"You play ball?" Wolfson asked.

"Some," Walker replied. "In high school."

Walker noted that in contrast to his angelic features, Wolfson's voice was pure New York City.

"These Phoenix guys play like the old Celtics or the Knicks of the 70's," Wolfson continued. "Remember how Walt Frazier and 'Dollar Bill' Bradley passed the ball four, six, eight times each possession? Waiting until a good shot became a great shot? Now if you're lucky it's maybe three passes and then some big white guy takes it to the rim. Used to be all back picks, figure eights, and screens."

"So beautiful it made you weep."

"Exactly." Wolfson sighed and turned the volume down.

"So what has Allan Singleton done now?"

"Nothing yet. His brother is concerned for his welfare."

"And you're trying to find him, is that it?"

"That's it."

Wolfson turned off the game and swiveled his chair to face Walker.

"How can I help? I haven't seen or heard from the guy in at least a year."

"Why did he leave the department? I'm told he had a promising career."

"He did," Wolfson answered. "Allan was on the cutting edge of making it easier for computers to talk to each other. His research was published in the leading journals."

"So what happened?"

"Allan was totally asocial, never pulled his weight around here, shirked faculty committee work—I had to cover for him and pick up the slack. For him, the job was about research, pure and simple. How much do you know about mathematics?"

"I can balance my checkbook."

"It's an incredibly arcane and narrow discipline," Wolfson sighed. "Beautiful, too. Like music, really. Sometimes you think you can hear the equations in your head. The problem is that the stuff we do can be used in a bunch of ways you can't even imagine. Your research can create programs to count human genomes or track the flight pattern of intercontinental ballistic missiles."

"Is that what got to Ted Kaczynski?"

"Give me a break," Wolfson chuckled. "I wasn't even here then. But some of the senior faculty who remember old Ted think he was nuts to begin with."

"Was Allan concerned about how his work would be used?"

"Sure. But he worried about a lot of things. You'd go into his office and you'd see stuff about the Animal Liberation Front on his wall, pictures of atrocities in the Middle East. It seemed to change every week."

"So he and Ted had some things in common."

"You want to know what I really think? Beneath all the political shit, he was first and foremost a scholar. The real deal."

"What do you mean?"

Wolfson leaned forward and smiled and Walker.

"Ever hear of Archimedes?"

"Perhaps in a past life."

"Archimedes was a famous third century B.C. mathematician who also designed war toys for the Romans. He believed in pure mathematics and detested engineers—called it 'a sordid and ignoble profession.' Archimedes was Allan's hero."

Walker watched as Wolfson's face became animated, his dark eyes flashing in his doughboy face.

"Allan got off on the game aspect of working out theories and equations. Once he solved something, he lost interest and immediately moved on to the next challenge. He never gave a thought about how his work might be used. Until he published his last article—about how computers talked to each other as I mentioned before."

"What happened?"

"I'm not sure. Suddenly he announced he was resigning. No explanation. No letter. He was gone in three days."

"Did he have any friends on the faculty?"

"You got to be kidding. This was a guy who never went to meetings or faculty events. People resented him for it."

"Girlfriends?"

"The man was a monk, Mr. Walker." He paused and began to rummage in his desk drawer. "Except for this." Wolfson handed Walker a matchbook. On the cover was a line drawing of a nude woman. Inside he read the address of a strip club on Market Street in San Francisco. "I found it in his drawer the week he moved out. Everybody has a secret life, I guess."

"May I keep this?"

"Be my guest."

Walker rose to go.

"One more thing, Professor. Do you think Allan is capable of violence?"

Wolfson smiled.

"The man I knew was a pussycat. But you never know about people. I mean, there's that matchbook, a whole secret life…"

Walker thanked him for his time and cooperation. As he left the office, he heard Wolfson click the volume back on. The rise and fall of the crowd noise followed Walker down the hall.

CHAPTER NINE

Cardboard fast food containers as sharp as missiles swirled and eddied at Walker's feet as he came around the corner into Market Street full into the teeth of a stiff wind. Squinting, he saw ahead a marquee that read *Live Nude Girls*. This once-proud stretch of San Francisco's main street had slid over the past half century into neglect and edgy grittiness. A block away, a bronze seal in the pavement marked the spot where the United Nations had been founded after World War II. Today, drifters and grifters criss-crossed the area, some with eyes hardened into the thousand-yard stare learned in Vietnamese rice fields or the main yard at San Quentin.

Somewhere in its past, the Market Street Cinema had been one of a number of movie theatres on the street, ranging from grand Moorish palaces to seedy yet functional second-run houses. Today, the only remnant of the Cinema's proud past was a powder-blue façade that resembled a mock castle. Walker passed under a series of crenellated arches' slits and approached a man in a raised booth. Without losing a beat, the man slid a cassette into a tape deck, said something unintelligible into a microphone—Walker guessed he was introducing the dancers onstage—and made change for Walker. His hand stamped and the change in his pocket, Walker pushed through a weathered swinging door and entered the theatre.

It was mid-afternoon and the Cinema was sparsely attended. Walker noticed some older pensioners scattered amidst a few office workers on their lunch hours, while one or two players from the suburbs wearing designer jeans and leather jackets tried but failed to hover unobtrusive along a railing to the rear. On stage, a somewhat plain-looking girl in her mid-twenties moved listlessly to recorded music. In her total nakedness, she seemed more vulnerable than erotic. Walker took a seat in the back row and waited.

The first dancer to approach him introduced herself as Felicia. She was in her late thirties, lanky and darkly attractive, wearing a champagne colored halter and matching panties. She began a practiced explanation of the various levels and prices for lap dances that Walker cut short by offering her a twenty to sit with him for ten minutes. Felicia's tongue darted across her lips, and Walker realized she must be tweaking on speed or crack. Before he could stop her, Felicia launched into a monologue about a planned trip to Hawaii, the latest book she was reading (about a pregnant woman with a transparent belly "so you could see the baby growing there"), and her 1987 280Z that she had rolled into a ditch last week. "It doesn't look so good now," she smiled.

Walker produced the picture of Allan Singleton, and with difficulty got Felicia to focus. "Everybody looks alike in here after a while," she murmured.

After Felicia left, Walker showed the picture to Lisa, a psychology graduate student from Louisiana with a sweet smile, and Porsche—spelled like the car, she carefully pointed out—a farm fresh blonde from Iowa with tired eyes. The responses were similar. Walker got up and walked out to the lobby and stood by the vending machines.

He noticed a sinewy brunette combing her hair in the reflection of one of the machines. The comb snapped through the thick mane that reached her mid-back. Walker caught her eye and moved closer.

"I'm looking for somebody," he began.

"Aren't we all." The voice had a slight accent. German or Israeli, Walker thought. Unlike the other dancers, she wore a knee-length organdy dress. Walker guessed her age as somewhere in her mid-forties—old for the business she was in despite her nicely-toned figure.

"Would you look at this for a moment?" Walker unfolded the picture once more.

She gave it a quick glance and her eyes narrowed into a frown.

"Yes, I know this man. So?"

"I need to talk to you about him."

"Why?"

"His brother is looking for him."

"I am about to end my shift."

"All right. Can I buy you lunch?"

The woman hesitated for a moment. Walker flashed what he hoped was his most engaging smile.

"Your friend used to come in a lot. Usually at noon when they lower the admission price for an hour."

The woman who had told him her name was Michaela sat across from him in the fly-specked Vietnamese luncheonette around the corner from the Cinema. "He hasn't been in all week."

"Did you ever talk to him?" Walker asked, dipping a soft spring roll in some sauce.

"People don't come to the Cinema to talk, my friend. Crystal could tell you more. He was her regular."

"Regular?"

"Repeat customer."

Walker brought the roll to his mouth. The taste paled in comparison to the dumplings at Sam Woo's. He thought of Linda. Michaela and Linda were roughly the same age, both liked Asian food. *Careful, Walker*, he told himself.

"Tell me about Crystal." He noticed that her eyes were cool and gray. They seemed to be appraising him as she sipped green tea from a chipped cup.

"Crystal is a baby," Michaela began. "She is one of the twenty-five-year-olds with cute little bodies who come to work here. They are, of course, attracted to the easy money. Before they know it, they are over thirty and other doors are closed to them."

Walker looked at the classic features of the woman sitting opposite him and imagined doors opening, not closing for her.

"How long have you worked there?"

"Too long." The cool eyes measured him again. "We are not here to talk about me. You want to know about Crystal."

"I'm listening if you want to talk."

"I'm your basic middle class Israeli girl, Mr....Walker." Michaela looked down at the business card that Walker had placed in her hand when they first sat down.

"Just Walker," he said.

"Walker. All right." She drew up her shoulders and leaned back in her chair. "I was a very idealistic young nursing student in Tel Aviv when the war in Lebanon broke out." She paused and looked at Walker. "You remember that war, Walker? Some Americans don't."

Walker nodded. Images from twenty years ago of jeeps with mounted fifty-caliber machine guns roaring through crumbling villages flooded his brain. The war of militias, of endless destruction—he remembered it well.

"After my country invaded the refugee camps in southern Lebanon, I lost my idealism. My job was to tend to those in the camps. It was truly horrible. I can't tell you what harm my people had done to unarmed civilians." She paused and looked down at her clasped hands. "I started taking valium to numb myself. Drugs were readily available in the hospitals. Eventually, I tried everything. I thought I could manage it, and for a while I did."

"Everything, meaning Heroin?"

"Yes. Heroin. It's a struggle, but I have been clean for five years. You've heard of the Bhagwan?"

"Of course." Walker recalled the free love guru whose devotees dressed in red clothes and bought him a dozen Rolls Royces. When the authorities managed to deport him to his native India, his followers became wandering samurais without a master.

"Many European druggies joined the group. After I came to the States, I went to their commune in Oregon and they locked me in a room for weeks and fed me and talked to me. Surprisingly, it worked. Or rather, I should say it is still working. One day at a time."

"I understand that a number of them became sex workers."

"Some women did indeed go into the sex industry precisely because it wasn't a stretch," Michaela continued. "After all, we had been trained by a master in the relationship between money and sex."

Walker smiled.

"The myth—the male myth to be precise—that sex workers are all highly sensual beings, priestesses and goddesses of love, is just bullshit," Michaela went on. "At the Cinema, at first it was interesting, even stimulating....all this endless foreplay. But after a while, it just became the rubbing of skin on skin. There are days when I don't show up for work or I leave early. Sometimes—rarely—something else besides money is exchanged with a customer."

Michaela held Walker's gaze for a beat before looking away.

"She has a room around the corner at the Hotel Seneca," Michaela said quickly.

"Crystal?"

"Yes. She is about five-two, platinum blonde, buxom, and wears Doc Martens."

Walker had taken out his reporter's notebook and was making entries. He looked up.

"Why?"

"Why what?"

"Why are you helping me?"

Michaela paused. "I don't know. Tell me I'm not going to regret it."

CHAPTER TEN

Walker had been here before. Not this precise hallway, not this particular hotel. But his work had taken him to many like it, all with the long, twisting corridors, stained carpets, and bathrooms at the end of the hall. Doors to be knocked on without knowing who or what was behind them. After leaving the restaurant, Walker had gone around the corner to the Seneca where a tall, turbaned Sikh deskman had given up Crystal's room number with minimal protestations. Walker had shown the man his P.I. license and had begun a yarn about the need to find a witness in a pending case when the man cut him off, consulted a list on the wall and wrote "312" on a slip of paper.

No one responded to Walker's repeated knocking and he left. Now two days later he was back, standing once more outside the door, listening. The compact weight of his Detective Special felt comforting in his inside jacket pocket. Sometimes you could tell when a room was empty—a settling floor board or a refrigerator sounded somehow different. The Seneca, however, was a Single Room Occupancy hotel, which meant no kitchens, no water pipes, and no refrigerators. Walker knocked. No response.

He knocked harder and the door nudged inward several inches. Walker sucked in his breath and pushed the door fully open. His hand slid inside his jacket to grab the butt handle of his gun. He took two quick steps inside.

The room was empty. It looked like an encampment that had been hastily abandoned or ransacked. A scarred bureau tilted crazily against one wall, its drawers gaping open. Various items of women's clothing were scattered on the floor and the bed sheets had been violently stripped from the mattress. Walker rummaged for a moment in the bureau drawers, finding a box of over-the-counter decongestant, an open packet of condoms and a handbill depicting the silhouette of a bucking horse that announced the annual rodeo at the Cow Palace. For reasons he didn't understand, Walker had always liked rodeos. He folded the handbill and tucked it in his pocket.

His toe came in contact with a small microwave oven resting on the rug. As he pushed it aside, he noticed a man's brown shoe. The shoe was attached to a foot that protruded from under the bed. Walker's knees wobbled and he felt the air leave his lungs.

Three long Yoga exhalations and inhalations cleared his head. Walker knelt by the bed and pushed it aside. The body of a very tall man lay crumpled on the floor. Walker knelt closer and stared at the lifeless face. He realized he was looking at Leather Pants, the man with the brown van.

There was remarkably little blood. Leather Pants had apparently been shot once at close range in the center of his chest. Walker noticed stippled powder burns on his shirt. He picked up the man's left arm and let it fall—no rigor mortis. Death was perhaps only hours old, at most half a day. Walker knew that the notion of a precise time of death was a myth kept alive in the movies: reputable pathologists recognized that most known tests—body temperature, eye fluid, and lividity—were notoriously fallible. Walker noted a gold band on the man's left ring finger. He ran his hands lightly over pants and jacket pockets until he found a billfold on the man's hip. A California driver's license yielded a name: Frank Quint. According to the card the dead man lived in a post office box.

Digging further into the wallet, Walker's fingers touched something familiar. He pulled out a second laminated card. Quint was the manager and sole proprietor of SUB-ROSA

INVESTIGATIONS, Inc., a state-licensed private eye firm that shared the man's P.O. Box. Walker had never heard of it.

Walker stood up and found a towel near the sink and busied himself smearing the door handle and any other surfaces he might have touched since entering the room. He felt woozy and his ears were ringing. Although he had encountered violent death in the course of his work, somehow each time it was new all over again.   Walker left the room and went out through the lobby into the street. The deskman was bent over a ledger and did not look up.

Walker went several blocks until he found a phone booth. He looked up the number for the Southern Precinct, dialed it, told the desk sergeant who answered that there was a dead body in room 312 at the Hotel Seneca, and hung up without leaving his name. Walker crossed the street to an anonymous neighborhood tavern. The interior darkness was cool and restorative, and he slid into a seat at the end of bar. He appeared to be the only customer. The barman took his order and placed two glasses in front of him on the bar. Walker carried the shot of brandy and a glass of ice water to a phone booth in the back of the room.

Walker pulled out his cell phone, dialed the Fairmont Hotel, and asked to be connected to David Singleton. After a long wait, a male voice that identified itself as Singleton's secretary came on the line. Walker told him he needed to speak to Singleton in person, that it was urgent. The secretary put him on hold for what seemed like an interminable amount of time. He finally came back on to say that Singleton could meet him at the hotel at 7:00 PM.

Walker leafed through the phone directory. As he expected, there was no residential listing for Quint. He was looking for a wife—or an ex-wife—someone who might open up about the dead detective. There were no persons named Quint in the entire city and county of San Francisco. He finished his drink, paid his tab and left the bar. Walker looked at his watch. Given afternoon traffic, it would take him nearly forty minutes to get home to his computer. The Civic Center and the Hall of Records were seven minutes away.

Walker crossed Market Street, cut through a bank parking lot, and saw the ornate black and gold dome of City Hall glinting through a dual row of   stunted and dusty Ginkgo trees. Breathing hard, he ran up the wide stone steps and entered the cool marble interior. He flipped open his laminated P.I. license, and passed quickly through the metal detector. Newlyweds posed for pictures with their relatives at the top of a sweeping staircase while a local politician Walker did not know was offering words to a microphone held by a reporter from a radio station. All around him, heels clicked on polished marble floors.

Walker entered the Recorder's Office, a high-ceilinged room lined with long desks where the microfiche and microfilm readers with contracts, documents, and real estate filings dating back to the Gold Rush could be retrieved and viewed. Everyone in the room—clerks and visitors alike—seemed to move at a stately, glacial pace, as if weighted down by history. Coming here, Walker often felt he had entered a Charles Dickens novel.

There were, however, some modern amenities. For newer records, the Recorder's Office had installed a bank of computers. Hoping that the record he wanted was stored in one of them, Walker sat down and typed Q-U-I-N-T into the index of the assessor's rolls. No one named Quint owned any property in the county of San Francisco. Next he accessed the registry of county marriage licenses. No hit.

Walker sighed. Either Quint was a bachelor, or had been married before the cut off date for computer records. Or the marriage was in another county, or perhaps out of state. Or he had been married once, but was now divorced. Walker knew that to check divorce filings, he would have to go the courthouse. He was running out of time and cursed himself that he had not gone home and used his own computer.

Walker scanned the service counter for a familiar face among the clerks. It was the sweater, not the features that he finally recognized. Bright white Christmas snowflakes against a green background, worn in stubborn defiance of the season by an angular, fortyish woman with pale-red hair. Walker could not remember her name, but he was certain she had worked there since the Flood.

As he approached the counter, Walker tried hard not to stare at the band-aid that held together the bridge of the woman's eyeglasses. Barbara—was that her name?—yes, Barbara—knew where to find a document when the microfiche had been eaten by an over-worked or poorly maintained viewing machine or an untrustworthy computer data entry system. He knew that without the woman's help, he could easily become lost in the Byzantine, Hapsburg Empire-like bureaucracy she presided over with a kind of loopy efficiency.

Walker wrote the name "Frank Quint" on a scrap of paper and told Barbara what he needed. Five minutes later, she returned with a photocopy of the dead detective's 1988 wedding license. He saw that the bride's maiden name had been Marsha Anderson.

Walker thanked Barbara profusely and copied the name into his notebook. Trying and failing to get a send signal on his cell phone, he rushed to a bank of phones under the main stairway to call Bruce Sullivan, a former co-worker he had first met a dozen years ago when he'd traded in his cab-driving job for an entry-level position with a local detective agency. Sullivan now ran his own service, which specialized in difficult locates and skip traces. Walker waited while Sullivan entered Quint's name into the professional license database and reported that the detective license had been revoked a year ago by the state-licensing agency. A woman named Marsha Quint was listed as his emergency contact and lived at an address in the Sunset District near the zoo.

Walker never really understood why they called it the Sunset District. Although located in western edge of the City, for most of the year the neighborhood remained buried in almost perpetual fog, the nearby ocean a distant dream, virtually invisible for days at a time. He had been surprised to read a magazine article that described the beach as a world class surfing destination. Prospective surfers, however, would find few amenities near the mud-gray municipal beach. Most of the houses that fronted the ocean looked barren and neglected. As Walker turned off Sloat Boulevard and approached the ocean, he saw red and orange streaks in the underside of a vast cloudbank in the western sky. He speculated that a real sunset was in progress somewhere behind the horizon.

Marsha Quint lived in a two-story pastel stucco complex that looked like someone's economy version of a 1950's beachfront motel. A forlorn date palm stood next to an entrance that was flanked by concrete posts studded with small stones and pieces of colored glass. Walker pushed a bell next to a nameplate and after a long moment was buzzed in.

He rode a slow, clanking elevator to the third floor. A woman stood in an open doorway at the end of the hall, watching Walker. She was strawberry blonde, on the far side of forty, and wore a flowered kimono robe.

"Yes?" she inquired.

On closer inspection, Walker saw that her face was better preserved than her figure, which appeared loose and shapeless beneath the kimono.

"It's about your husband," Walker began.

Marsha Quint looked back into the room. Walker saw a sun-colored couch in the far corner of the room where a shirtless twenty-something young man with spiky yellow hair lounged.

"It's always about my husband," she sighed. "What's he done now?"

"It might be better if this were private," Walker said, nodding toward the young man.

She turned back into the room. "Why don't you go outside and play, Artie?"

The man addressed as "Artie" pulled on a sweatshirt with lettering reading Accordions *Don't Play Lady of Spain, People Do.* He picked up a guitar case and pushed past Walker and Mrs. Quint into the hallway, his face sullen and hard. Walker noticed a smudge of lipstick near the corner of his mouth.

Walker followed Marsha Quint into the room and sat on the couch, immediately sinking into the cavity left by Artie's body. He struggled to right himself as she settled across from him in a canary-yellow canvas director's chair.

"I'm in the same business as your husband," Walker said and handed her his business card. She stared at it with complete lack of interest.

There was no getting around it, Walker thought.

"Your husband was killed, Mrs. Quint. He was shot dead in a hotel room on Sixth Street."

Marsha Quint's lower face quivered and fell apart. Her hand clutched her kimono at her neck.

"My God..."

"I'm sorry to be the one to tell you," Walker continued. He got up and looked quickly around. Seeing an open off-brand bottle of Scotch on the kitchen counter, he found a glass that was not too smeared, poured a stiff drink, and handed it to her. She downed it in a gulp.

"Were you working with him?" Her voice was a hoarse whisper.

"Not exactly. Let's say our paths crossed."

"We've been separated for a year. He's a total shit. But I never expected..."

"Did he have a partner? Any staff?"

"Frank? No, it was all front with him."

Walker thought of his own one-man home office and realized he and Quint might have more in common than he would care to acknowledge.

"Did he ever talk about his cases?"

"Frank always had a mouth on him, but his cases were the one thing he would never talk about."

Walker noticed that her voice was slurred now and the corners of her mouth were pulled into an almost wistful, manic smile.

"When was the last time you spoke with him?"

"Ten days ago, maybe. I called him because he was late again with the alimony." The smile had suddenly turned bitter.

"What is it, Mrs. Quint?" Walker prompted.

"He told me he was about to come into some really big money very soon. Some irony, huh?"

"Do you know what he meant?"

"No idea." She got up and replenished her glass. "He always claimed he had something going, some hot lead. Most of the time it was just smoke. This was probably no different."

Silence enfolded the room. Walker became aware of a window rattling from a breeze coming off the ocean.

"I understand your husband was having some trouble with his license."

"I don't know." Mrs. Quint blew her nose. "Something about an unauthorized entrance. They said he kicked in a door, I think. Big deal."

Walker rose from the couch. She looked like she was about to fall apart again.

"Is there someone you could call—someone who could come over and be with you?"

"Artie'll be back soon." She wiped her cheek with the back of her right hand. "I'll be fine."

Walker let himself out and left the building. In the gathering twilight, he saw the young man in question hunched over the engine of a rust-stained VW bus. Artie appeared to be regapping its spark plugs. A chipped surfboard poked out of a window. Walker slid into the seat of his car and drove off without looking back. He glanced at his watch. Walker knew that by using the pay phone to call the police he had only carved himself a small slice of time before the police would identify him by working backward from the Widow Quint to the hotel clerk. It was not a comforting thought.

It was completely dark by the time he parked in the Fairmont Hotel garage. Walker took the elevator to the top floor and found David Singleton's suite at the end of a long wood-paneled hallway. The door was opened by Singleton himself. He wore faded jeans and a blue Brooks Brothers button-down dress shirt. He led Singleton to a cluster of leather sofas fronting a working fireplace. Pale flames shot up from what Walker guessed were seasoned Madrone logs. The men sat facing each other, a chrome and glass Art Deco coffee table between them. Singleton put his feet up on the table and Walker noticed he was wearing soft moccasins and no socks. As before, Singleton's designer eyeglasses hung from his neck on a chain.

"I'm afraid your brother is in trouble," Walker began.

Singleton listened intently as Walker recounted his visit to the Seneca Hotel and his conversation with Marsha Quint. When Walker was finished, Singleton placed his feet on the ground and squared his body.

"You think Allan is responsible for this Quint person's death?"

"I don't know. It's a possibility we can't ignore."

"Jesus Christ."

"Your brother is on the move," Walker continued. "He definitely seems capable of violence. It means that now we have to take his threat to Harrison Bledsoe much more seriously."

"This does change things," Singleton responded, fingering his eyeglass chain.

"It might help me find Allan if I knew why he choose Bledsoe in the first place."

"Bledsoe's a buccaneer capitalist, a prominent figure."

"There's got to be more to it than that."

"Harrison Bledsoe has been incredibly adept at a creating a benevolent image of himself as some kind of New Age country store keeper. People forget the numerous offshore sweatshops that produce the stuff he sells. That alone would piss Allan off mightily."

"What makes him special? Bledsoe certainly can't be only the rich person running that kind of game."

"His foundations. Even the feds gave up figuring out what some of his non-profits really do. Or they don't care. Rumor has it when his father ran the company, one of the family's foundations was a cover in the arms-for-hostages deal back under Reagan. Nobody could prove it, though."

"We need to find your brother before more people get hurt."

Walker thought of the late 1960's and the Madison, Wisconsin, bombing of the math building. All that rage, anger.

Allan had been there. The times were different, but perhaps the same hot flame continued to rage in the furnace inside Allan Singleton's head.

David Singleton adjusted his glasses on the bridge of his nose.

"What do you suggest?"

"That you provide Bledsoe's security people with Allan's picture."

"Is it necessary for them to know about what happened at that hotel?"

"If you don't tell them and something happens to Bledsoe you are an accessory before the fact. Not a good idea."

Walker was not sure that what he had just said was accurate, but it sounded good. He wished Singleton would stop fidgeting with his glasses. The man worked the chain as if it were a rosary.

"I can't really do my job properly and do damage control at the same time."

"I appreciate that, Walker. But it's my brother we are talking about here."

"I understand. I can try to keep things under wraps, but I don't for how long."

"What do you mean?"

"Well, there's Quint's widow and the hotel desk clerk," Walker continued. "When the police talk to them, they might decide they like me for the shooter."

Singleton stopped playing with the chain and looked up at Walker.

"Would you tell them about Allan?"

"I'd try to keep him out of it, but there are no guarantees that they wouldn't find out anyway. The police are going to question people at the hotel about visitors to the girl's room. They could pressure her and she might crack."

Walker wondered how long he would hold out if he were the one being squeezed. At the very least, he saw his license going out the window if he didn't cooperate. In the worst case, he could be charged with homicide. He wondered if David Singleton would care. He decided not to ask.

"All right," Singleton sighed. "I'll call Bledsoe's people in the morning."

Singleton rose and accompanied Walker to the door.

"I imagine when you took this assignment you had no idea it would turn into something like this." He rearranged his face into a forced smile and took Walker's hand.

Walker smiled and said nothing. He returned Singleton's grip and left the suite.

As he left the parking garage, the lights from oncoming cars puddled and haloed on his windshield. Walker rubbed his eyes; he needed to get home, he needed to think. Most of all, he needed a drink.

CHAPTER ELEVEN

Walker got home a little before 9:30 and made himself two fried egg sandwiches on wheat toast. He fed Archie some pieces of bacon and settled into his window chair with the sandwich and a glass of Bacardi and Diet Coke balanced on his lap. Archie made erratic stabs at what was for him, as well as Walker, a late dinner. The room was dark, the only illumination coming from the fish bowl that Walker had lit from behind with a track light. Watching Archie spin and twist as he grabbed a piece of bacon made Walker think of a tiny biplane performing barrel rolls against a bright August sky.

Walker rose and went to the computer, flipped it on. He skimmed through a news index header search for Allan Singleton. He had already performed this search at the beginning of the assignment, but he wanted to make sure he hadn't overlooked anything, particularly references to the Madison bombing. He found none. Walker was about to close down the search when he came across a 1957 article from Saranac Lake, New York, describing a fire at the Singletons' summer residence, known as Loon Lake. Both parents died in the blaze. State police investigators interviewed the boys, then ages twelve and eight, about the fire; their initial focus had been on Allan, the younger of the two, as an arson suspect. David was able to convince them that the fire had been an accident. The event, Walker realized, must have been cataclysmic in the lives of these young boys. He noticed that David Singleton had named his first start up company after the family home.

Walker turned off the computer. He wondered why such a horrific event had not brought the brothers closer to each other, why it hadn't prevented their final drifting apart. On the other hand, the fire and the loss of his parents could have been the original trigger of Allan's mental break with the world. Why had David Singleton held back this information? Walker wondered if there had been more to the fire than what the investigators had gleaned. Could Allan have been involved after all and was David covering for him all these years? It seemed entirely possible.

Walker looked over at Archie again and realized it was time to examine his situation, to peer into his own fish bowl. Each of his cases had pushed him into a corner. Walker didn't even know Allan Singleton; he was just someone he had been hired to find. And now he found himself trying to buy time for a person he had never even met, someone who might in fact be a killer. Could it be that he subconsciously felt sympathetic towards Allan Singleton? If not with his methods, then with some of his goals? After all, the man was against inequality and oppression, and he seemed to want a more just world—ideas and ideals by no means alien to Walker. The rum was going down too all easily and Walker knew he was on the near edge of drunkenness.

Thinking about his other case, Walker realized he was refusing to acknowledge his client might have carefully planned the brutal murder of his own sister. So what if Ali Bakkrat played chess and was a sensitive human being? It didn't mean Walker could ignore the clear possibility that his client was a cool, calculating killer—Ali's undeniable access to the murder weapon certainly suggested planning and premeditation.

Walker drained his glass and poured another. The two cases had somehow come to exist for him in the same crazed parallel universe. His sense of allegiance and the reactions it prompted had been instinctive. That was the trouble, Walker told himself; had he submitted his actions to even minimal reflection, he would not be in the tight corner he now found himself.

No, that was not true, either, he realized. He had understood from the beginning what was at a stake and still chose to act the way he did. He knew it could be argued that he was merely following the bedrock code of his profession— unwavering loyalty to one's client. But was it also that Walker, who had always lived on the margins of respectability himself, found himself continually drawn to defending people who themselves were on the edge and cast out by society? Walker knew that if you did the job right, the answers to these questions might not matter in the end. He also recognized that this knowledge might be of little use in the short run.

The doorbell jerked Walker away from these circular thoughts and out of his chair. He opened the door and peered down the steps. Although he should have been, he wasn't surprised to see Michaela, the Israeli dancer from the Cinema, coming up the stairs, her face pale against a dark raincoat worn belted at the waist. She gave him a small, tight smile as she entered the apartment.

"You always live in the dark like this?" Michaela asked, taking in the room and the back-lit fish bowl.

"Only when I'm drinking." Walker smiled wearily and came up behind her to help her off with her coat.

"I'm scared, Walker."

She sat on the couch, hugging her knees.

"What's wrong?" Walker asked.

He poured some rum into a fresh glass and handed it to her. Michaela gulped it down.

"Crystal called me tonight from Reno. She said there was a dead man in her room."

"Yes, I know. I was the one who found him."

"My God, Walker," she gulped down the rum. She held out her glass and Walker refilled it.

"Tell me what Crystal said."

"She came home from the Cinema last night and discovered this strange dead person on her floor." Michaela greedily drank from the glass and continued. "She was terrified. She had never seen him before. She panicked and called her boyfriend, Allan. He came over, looked at the dead man, and gave her some money to get out of town for a few days."

"Did she say if Allan seemed surprised?"

"According to Crystal, no. That's what scared her."

"What did he say?"

"He thought someone might be looking for him." Michaela put down the glass and hugged her knees again.

"Anything else?"

"Allan gave her something he wanted her to hide. Some kind of computer disc."

Walker looked hard at her.

"Did he say anything about what was on the disc?"

"No." Warmth was beginning to appear in Michaela's cheeks. "Crystal took it, but she was scared. She thought the disc may have had something to do with getting this man killed. She gave it to me and told me to get rid of it."

Walker was out of his seat, kneeling next to Michaela. His hand gripped her forearm, fingers unconsciously pressing into her skin.

"Do you still have it?"

Michaela's widening eyes made Walker realize he was hurting her. He drew back his hand.

"I put it in my locker at the Cinema," Michaela replied, rubbing her forearm.

"I want you to get it. Tonight, if possible."

"I don't know, Walker."

"Why not?"

"It's dangerous. People have been killed."

"No one knows you have it."

"Crystal knows. Besides, it's too late—the Cinema is closed until ten o'clock tomorrow morning."

"Do it then. Please." Walker stood up and moved to the window. He stared out at the bay for a moment before turning back to Michaela.

"I'm sorry. I didn't mean to come on like gangbusters," he confided. "I'm trying to prevent more people from getting killed."

Michaela stretched and yawned.

"I'm too tired to think right now, Walker."

"All right."

Walker went to his closet and began to pull out sheets and blankets.

"You can spend the night on the couch. We'll deal with this in the morning."

Michaela nodded, her face blank. He handed a clean tee-shirt to her and she meandered towards the bathroom with it hanging over her shoulder. Walker made up the couch. Michaela returned five minutes later with her hair combed out, wearing the tee-shirt, which fell mid-thigh on her. She slid between the sheets and smiled up at Walker.

"You're nice for a detective."

"Thank you. Get some sleep now." Walker turned out Archie's light and went into his bedroom. He undressed and got in bed where his mind raced and for the first time in years, he thought about having a cigarette. Alcohol and stress hormones porpoised through his veins until his conscious mind let go and he fell into a shallow sleep.

Walker dreamt he entered—floated, really—into a large Baroque ballroom where soft violin music played. Empty folding chairs were set in front of a raised podium where two men sat facing each other over a chess board. Walker moved nearer. In one chair, Ali Bakkrat was hunched over his pieces, his chin cupped in his hand. He smiled at Walker and soundlessly introduced him to the man opposite him: *my friend Allan Singleton.* Walker peered at the man only to discover that a hood shrouded his face.

A deep shudder passed through Walker's body. Gradually, the shivering was replaced by a warmness beginning to radiate throughout his body from his buttocks and lower back. He felt the feathery weight of an arm encircling him and a smooth palm resting on his belly. A compartmentalized dreamer, Walker heard the observer who always commented on his dreams inform him that Linda's self-imposed exile had ended, that all was forgiven between them. Cool, tapered fingers began to knead and caress his stomach. Another part of his brain told him to wake up, that this was not Linda. Walker fell back into the world. He saw dark strands of hair breaking liking a frozen wave over his forearm. Michaela's mouth found his. Walker started to fall back into the void again.

"This is not a good idea," Walker said, pulling away.

Michaela said nothing and looked at him.

Streaks of morning light nibbled at the edge of the window blind. Walker got up, found his bathrobe and disappeared into the kitchen. Pots and pans banged. He lit the gas ring and began to make campfire coffee.

Michaela rose, straightened Walker's tee-shirt, which had bunched at her waist, and walked into the kitchen. She sat quietly at the table.

Walker brought a steaming cup to her, placing it on the counter.

"Why did you do that?"

"You shouldn't have to ask," Michaela replied, her lips tentatively testing the rim of the cup. "I like you."

Walker pulled a chair around and sat facing her.

"Who exactly are you?"

"I already told you."

"What else are you?"

"You might say I'm your counterpart."

"What the hell are you talking about?"

"I'm a spy, Walker."

"Sure. Why not?"

"It wasn't something I chose, exactly."

"I see. You just answered a want ad?" Walker fought to control his growing exasperation.

"Try to listen, will you please? After I left the commune in Oregon," she began, "I was completely broke and decided to come to San Francisco. I quickly found out that my Israeli nursing license was worthless in California—I could get a job drawing blood, but that was about it. So I went to the consulate here, ready to beg airfare to get home. To my total surprise, a man who called himself a trade attaché offered me a job. He said they thought some local businesses owned by Arabs were siphoning cash to the PLO. One of the businesses was the

Cinema. They wanted me to get a job on the inside and see what I could learn."

"Go on."

"At first it sounded like fun in a way and no big deal," Michaela continued. "I thought they would give me a job as a cashier or something, but the manager immediately hired me as a dancer. Within a week I saw that the owners weren't political at all—the cash they skimmed from the business wasn't going anywhere but into their own pockets."

Michaela shifted in the chair and curled her legs under her.

"There were a lot of drugs around, and pretty soon I fell back into using. It was a familiar emotional space for me. Too familiar. I began to make up stories for the people at the consulate. It was easy figuring out what they wanted to hear: the night manager calling for a cab, putting a paper bags full of cash being in the back seat, telling the driver to go to airport where someone would take the package, that kind of thing. They bought it all. I made their little skimming operation sound like something out of James Bond. I just thought I was buying a little more time before they found out that I was scamming them, but they actually believed everything. One senior guy even offered me a lieutenant's commission in the Israeli army. Soon I was given material to read—intelligence reports, background briefings...I refused the commission, of course. That would have been totally ridiculous." Michaela's voice trailed off.

"That's it?"

"Pretty much. Yes."

"Interesting story. Why are you telling it to me?"

"Okay..." Michaela hesitated. "I'll be totally honest. I need your help."

"Is that why you tried to fuck me?"

"No. Well, in part, yes." She paused again. "But it was not something I had to force myself to do. I wasn't lying when I said I liked you."

"What kind of help?"

"I want to get out, Walker."

"All right. How do I fit in?"

"You could be my insurance policy. You're my proof that I exist, that I am who I say I am."

"Why don't you go to a neutral embassy or to a foreign newspaper? You don't need me."

"I'm not ready to see my name in lights, Walker. I just want my life back."

Walker took the cups to the sink and rinsed them.

"It's almost morning. What do you usually have for breakfast?"

"Anything. Eggs. Will you help me?"

Walker broke several brown eggs into a bowl and beat them with a wire whip.

"We can talk about that later. First, get me the disc."

"I see...a bargain." Michaela's smile was thin and taut. "I do something for you and you return the favor...is that how it will play out?"

"You could call it that."

Walker slid two halves of a sliced English muffin into the bottom of the broiler and lit the oven.

Michaela stared at Walker for a long moment, got up, and moved away in the direction of the bathroom. Within moments, Walker heard the shower running.

CHAPTER TWELVE

Walker wove through the mid-morning wash of pedestrians on Market Street, looked over his shoulder at a streetcar bogged down in traffic a block behind him, and ducked under the golden arches of the corner Mickey D franchise. He made his way to the counter and ordered a small coffee. Drumming his fingers on the counter, Walker watched a heavyset man in a soiled army jacket and the fur hat of a Russian prince order a cup of hot water, which he took to a table where he produced his own tea bag. The man's eyes followed Walker as he hurried to a seat by the window in time to see Michaela step down from the streetcar and wait on the traffic island for the light to change. After a moment, she crossed Market and entered the Cinema.

Walker quickly scanned the street for anyone who seemed out of place or too interested in Michaela. Nothing. Michaela had argued over breakfast that she did not want him to accompany her when she retrieved the disc. Walker reluctantly agreed, but decided it would be prudent to watch her back. Tailing Michaela in the morning commuter crush had not been easy—she had walked up Columbus Avenue to Market, where without warning, she stepped aboard an outbound vintage streetcar. Fearful of being seen if he boarded with her, Walker opted to half-walk, half-run on the sidewalk. He remembered reading a feature article in the paper some years ago in which a reporter wagered that he could get to the foot of Market from the Civic Center before the streetcar arrived. The reporter had been wrong, but only by a few minutes. Walker lucked out when Michaela's streetcar ground to a halt in traffic a block before the Cinema.

He got out his cell phone, dialed a number and was placed on hold. He sipped from the coffee cup he held in his other hand. The coffee was scalding and tasted of cardboard. He thought of the pot he had brewed for himself and Michaela hours earlier, and her revelations about herself and her work at the Cinema. He realized that if she had been telling the truth, her retrieval of the disc might be putting her into even further jeopardy. He would have to stay close to her. Walker's party came on the line.

"Arnie? It's Walker."

"I was going to call you next week, *boychick*. Getting to be renewal time for your Errors and Omissions floater."

Walker remembered that it was indeed time to renew the liability policy that protected him from some of the more egregious blunders a private eye could make and for which he could be sued. He assured the insurance agent that the check had just gone out in the mail and went on to explain the true nature of his call. Arnie went off the line for several minutes before coming back with the information Walker had requested.

"Steak's on me next week at Izzy's," Walker responded, scribbling in his notebook before breaking the connection.

Walker left the restaurant and walked back toward North Beach. Michaela had agreed to return to Walker's place with the disc after her shift at the Cinema. That gave him several hours before he would have to follow her again. This time he would use a "front tail," which meant walking ahead of the subject, keeping track of the person's reflected image in store windows and in the outer edges of his own extra-wide dark glasses. Not easy, but still possible. With any kind of luck, he would arrive home before her with time to spare.

The man Walker wanted was not in the first three North Beach cafes he entered. Finally, Walker found him seated in the back of the Trieste hunched over a chess board under a faded sepia-tinted mural of musicians at a Mediterranean seaside village. Walker bought a caffé latte at the counter and slid it in front of the tall bearded man.

"For me? Hell, you haven't even lost yet, Walker."

"I'm not here to play, Michael." Walker sat down across from him.

The man sipped the coffee and nodded approvingly. For the twenty or so years Walker had known Michael Botin, he had always worn some version of the same blue chambray work shirt and soft leather vest hanging loosely on his lanky frame. Botin was a North Beach fixture: a full-time poet, part-time longshoreman and master chess player. He claimed he learned the game in the forecastle of a Merchant Marine ship during the last days of the Korean War. Pushing seventy, his face was clear and unlined.

When work on the large cargo ships crossed the bay to Oakland in the 1970's, Botin and his fellow dock workers laid claim to the pensions their leader Harry Bridges had skillfully negotiated in return for allowing the ship owners to mechanize the San Francisco waterfront. Botin still worked two or three days a month, when the work was there. Mostly, he played chess and wrote poetry. Walker had seen some of the poetry and liked what he had read.

"This is Roberto, he waits tables at the Roma." Botin gestured to a dark-skinned young man in his twenties wearing a white pressed shirt sitting across from him. Roberto nodded without looking up and shoved a pawn forward on the chessboard.

Walker consulted his notebook.

"Michael, were there any tournaments say within a hundred and fifty miles three weekends ago, on the twenty-second through the twenty-fourth of the month?"

"Probably." Botin's attention had shifted to the chess board. Roberto's pawn was threatening his rook.

"I need to know."

"Great Scott, Walker. You *are* a wonder. Want the world to come to your door." The older man smiled, revealing nicotine-stained teeth.

"Come on, Michael."

"Help yourself." Botin unfastened the straps on a worn leather briefcase—Walker thought of school children in a Norman Rockwell painting trudging through snow drifts on their way to a one-room school house—and handed Walker several well-thumbed chess magazines. Botin turned back to the board and moved his rook out of danger.

Using his finger to trace paragraphs, Walker worked his way laboriously through interviews, articles on tournaments, and advertisements for ornamental chess pieces. After twenty minutes, he found what he wanted and handed the magazines to Botin, who slid them back into his briefcase. Walker eyed the chess board. Both men were in the mid-game and appeared to have lost an even number of pieces. Walker looked at his watch, debated with himself for a moment, and bolted toward the door.

Walker sat across from Delucca in the attorney's office. The window blinds were closed as before and the mid-afternoon sun scattered shadows on the floor like spokes of a wheel. Delucca was in shirtsleeves, his suspenders unhooked and hanging loosely at his waist. He listened intently as Walker spoke.

"Ali was out of town the weekend the uncle reported the gun stolen."

"Where? Doing what?"

"In Stockton. At a chess tournament."

"Are you certain?"

"Yes. I saw his name in a list of contestants in a magazine."

"Sure of the date?"

"Yes. It matches the date I got from an insurance agent who owes me a favor."

"Interesting. Where does this take us?"

"Right to Hassan Bakkrat." Walker's voice was tense, hard. "What if Hassan took or stole the gun from his brother, gave it to Ali and convinced him somehow that it was his familial or religious duty to punish Noor for betraying the family?"

"That's pretty extreme, Walker."

"This whole case is extreme, Malcolm." Walker went to the window and looked out at the shopping center. He realized he needed to hit a home run today with this lawyer.

"Hassan Bakkrat was the one obsessed with Noor," Walker continued. "Not Ali."

"How do you know?"

"Bakkrat's brother told me."

"We can't use it. Hearsay."

"I'm not finished."

Delucca patted his pockets for his cigarette pack. Walker began to pace in front of the window—he found he thought more clearly if he could not see the lawyer's eyes boring in on him.

"Hassan is pulling all the strings."

"I'm listening."

"Remember how concerned he was that Ali be tried as a minor? What if Bakkrat, who is a smart man, knew damn well that if Ali were the shooter, he'd be tried as a minor? What if he knew he'd only do chump-change time in jail?"

"Hell, if you were the kid's father, you wouldn't want your son tried as an adult either." Delucca crushed out his cigarette in an ashtray.

"Stay with me on this, Malcolm. What did Ali do right after the shooting?" Walker continued, spacing out his words. "He walks down the hall and...gives...the gun...to...*his father*. He doesn't hang on to it, he doesn't throw it away—he gives it *back* to the person who gave it to him."

"Maybe. Or you could argue that he was simply surrendering, giving himself up." Seeing Walker frown, Delucca shrugged and smiled.

"Hey, what you've come up with is good. It's just not enough."

"What more would you like, short of a confession?"

"Well, something resembling a motive would be good. Fundamentalist fanaticism won't take us very far. Remember, Hassan told us he is not that religious."

"I know. There's more."

"What?"

"I don't know yet."

On his way out, Walker thought of the New York of his youth and Con Ed construction barriers that used to read: *Dig We Must*. He knew he had no choice but to keep shoveling, even if it meant burying his client's father. If he was wrong, Walker knew Delucca would never hire him again. He would be branded as the investigator who burned one client to save another.

Walker inserted the disc into the drive and waited while it thrummed, clattered and came to life. Michaela sat close to him, her eyes unwavering and intent on the computer screen. Numbers and letters cascaded into view. Out of the seemingly random pattern, a long series of equations flowed down the screen. After several long minutes, Walker rubbed his eyes and rose from his chair.

"It will take a computer geek to make sense of this," Michaela sighed.

She rose from her chair.

"I know someone who could take a look at it…"

"That's all right. I may have just the right guy for this." Walker thought of Toby Wolfson, Allan's former colleague.

He switched off the computer.

Michaela put on her coat.

"Cold?" Walker inquired.

Michaela moved toward him and took his head in both her hands.

"No, not cold." She kissed him lightly on the forehead. "I have to go now."

Walker looked closely at Michaela. Her irises were like saucers. "What did you take?" he demanded.

"A little speed. Not much." Michaela pulled the coat around her. "I have to work a double shift tonight."

Walker wondered how long she had been high. The tail job back from the Cinema had been uneventful. Michaela had not stopped and had gone straight to Walker's. He guessed she scored the dope at the Cinema.

"Your getting high—did it have anything to do with what happened between us last night?"

"Don't be silly, Walker. I told you—I have a double shift."

Michaela stood at Walker's desk, looking down at some sheets of paper resting in his printer out bin—a *Memo to File* Walker had been working on about Hassan Bakkrat.

"Please don't read that," Walker said. He stepped closer and turned the pages over.

"The Bakkrat name is well known in Palestine. Ahmed Bakkrat in particular."

"So I've heard."

Walker walked to the door and held it open.

"He was killed by an Israeli rocket and is considered a martyr." Michaela moved to the door and paused in front of Walker. "Of course, as with all legends, the truth is always somewhat more nuanced."

Michaela moved through the doorway, but Walker caught her roughly by the arm.

"Tell me what you know."

"It's not important, Walker. Michaela smiled and disengaged her arm from his grip. "Perhaps we can discuss it later when you trust me a little more."

She started down the steps. Walker stood in the doorway until she reached the front entrance where she paused to blow him a kiss. Then she was gone. After a long moment, he closed the door and went back inside.

Walker returned to his desk and ejected the Allan Singleton's disk from the computer. He wondered where the former math professor was tonight. The Harrison Bledsoe speech was three days away and everything pointed to Allan's potential to do harm. Quint's death suggested he'd moved on from the rhetoric of violence to violence of the deed. If Walker could find him before Bledsoe's speech perhaps more carnage could be averted. Allan must be near—the event would keep him tethered to the city. Somewhere safe, anonymous.

The image of a rearing, bucking horse ridden by a cowboy floated into Walker's consciousness. Where he had seen that before?

Walker got up, turned on the light, went to his desk, and dug around in his middle drawer until he found the rodeo advertisement he had taken from Singleton's hotel room. At the bottom of the cheaply-printed handbill, beneath the image of the rider's spurred heel, Walker read in small block letters: *Rodeo Motel 3235 Geneva Avenue Off-Season Rates for the Commercial Traveler.* He saw in his mind's eye the sparsely populated southeastern edge of the city and the stretch of Geneva where it butted into Old Bayshore Boulevard at the county line. The geography was especially confusing: one block of Geneva might lie within San Francisco while the next could be in Daly City. Walker guessed that the Rodeo Motel was one of several look-alike motels located within lasso distance of the Cow Palace, the site of the annual rodeo. Except for Rodeo Week, the motels were usually empty.

Walker undressed and climbed into bed. It was a long shot, but it was the only one he had.

CHAPTER THIRTEEN

Walker parked next to a brick utility substation on Geneva Avenue across from the motel and got out for a closer look. A few straggly pepper trees and one stunted palm provided only minimal shade and the late morning sun was already bearing down hard on the single-story building. From the look of its weathered exterior, Walker guessed the Rodeo Motel had been baking in the same hot sun since the 1950's. A red neon replica of the bucking horse and rider from the handbill reared over the front entrance. He waited for a large tanker truck to pass, then crossed the street and went into the office.

Several inexpensive reproductions of famous paintings of the Old West by Frederic Remington leaned against a scarred counter next to a stack of what in an earlier decade would have been called Danish modern chairs. Walker was struck by the smell of fresh paint and old linoleum. A man on stepladder wearing a dark sweatshirt reading "NYFD" with a paint roller in his hand turned to look at Walker. He had sallow features, an aquiline nose, and a gold-capped front tooth. Walker guessed the man was Asian or Latin.

The man slowly backed down the ladder and put the paint roller down. Standing behind the counter, he wiped his fingers carefully on a newspaper. Apparently, he was the day desk clerk, not just a handyman.

"I'm looking for someone," Walker began, pulling out his picture of Allan Singleton and placing it on the counter.

The clerk fingered the photo for a moment. Walker watched a blot of fresh paint appear in one corner. Somewhere an air conditioning unit rumbled to life. Walker waited. The clerk looked up from the photo and said something in a language Walker thought could be Tagalog.

Since the Philippines had once been ruled by Spain, Walker reasoned he might as well dredge up whatever remained of his high school Spanish.

"*Este hombre es mi hermano. Mi companero,*" Walker laboriously enunciated. "*Conosco esta persona?*"

The clerk, apparently unaffected by three centuries of Spanish rule, stared blankly back at Walker. His patience evaporating like a cold soft drink on a hot day, Walker went into full charade mode.

He quickly tilted forward and placed the heels of each palm flat against his cheeks, fingers wiggling and flailing in front of his face. Walker's upper body moved vigorously from side to side. The man shrugged. Seemingly from nowhere, the chorus from the Coaster's hit single from Walker's high school days rocketed into his head and out of his mouth: "*I been searchin'...searchin'...searchin' every which way.*"

The clerk's eyes widened and he glanced furtively towards the key rack behind him.

"*Noh Yin,*" the clerk mumbled.

"What?

Raising his voice as if addressing a child or deaf person, the clerk repeated the two words for Walker.

"*NOH YIN.*"

No in. Singleton indeed had a room, but was not in it.

Walker knew the clerk would not easily give up the room number. Establishments like the Rodeo Motel offered their tenants the unstated yet implicit assurance that they would be protected from bill collectors, bondsmen, and ex-wives. It was good for business and preserved the motel's reputation as a kind of Foreign Legion pit stop for travelers with carefully nurtured low profiles. In the movies one might slip the room clerk a twenty, but Walker knew that here at the Rodeo Motel, that ploy would just arouse more suspicion and he would as likely be given deliberate misinformation.

He made a writing motion with his hand and the clerk gave him a copy of the motel handbill and a pencil stub. Hunching over the counter and using his forearm as a shield, Walker laboriously etched out several carefully-penned X's and O's. He folded the paper twice and handed it to the clerk. Walker found his oversized dark glasses and put them on. The clerk made no move to place the message in any of the numbered slots behind him. The man's eyes stayed on Walker as he moved towards the door. Just as he reached for the handle, Walker saw in the image reflected in his glasses the clerk drop the message into a numbered slot. Walker let out his breath as the door closed behind him. While standing at the counter pretending to write his note, he had memorized the pigeonholes into a grid pattern. The clerk had left the message in square number seventeen: Walker's high school football jersey number. *A karmic convergence,* Walker speculated. *Thank you, Coasters.*

He walked east on Geneva towards Old Bayshore Boulevard. At the corner he turned left and cut through a self-service gas station to double back along the alley that ran parallel to the motel. Broken glasses crunched under his feet and the sun bore down on his back. Walker removed his jacket and wiped his brow.

Coming up on the building from behind, he found Allan's unit without much trouble. After listening at the door for several long moments, he knocked and waited. Nothing. Walker tried the door. Locked. It felt like a dead bolt. A credit card would be of no use.

Walker went to the rear of the unit. The wood around the window stop was rotted and pitted and gave without much pressure. In a moment, Walker was inside.

His eyes fought to adjust to the sudden dimness. The air was thick and heavy and the sudden influx of light from the open window bathed the walls in a greenish wash. Above his head in one corner, the dead fish eye of a TV set chained to one wall added to the feeling of entering an underwater aquarium.

The center of the room was dominated by a double bed covered with a wrinkled, mustard-colored spread. Socks and underwear still in their cellophane wrappings lay in neatly arranged stacks on the bed. Along with a pair of fresh chino pants and an empty plastic laminated holder, the kind used to identify conventioneers. There was also an open packet of pushpins and a spool of red thread.

A relatively new model laptop computer stood on the one table in the room next to a frayed sports jacket hanging from a chair. Walker turned it on. As he expected, the machine would not engage the operating system without a password. He shut it down and turned his attention to the walls. A large portable portfolio, the kind Walker had often seen artists and models carry on the streets of Manhattan, was propped against the far wall. When Walker untied the shoelace cord that held the two halves together, the case fell open and Walker saw both surfaces were covered with newspaper articles and clippings fastened with pushpins. Red thread looped over the pushpins fanned out in several directions like stark arterial highways. Walker moved closer. A surge of adrenalin shot through his veins as he realized he might be looking at a three-dimensional road map of Allan Singleton's deepest obsessions.

A number of articles dealt with recent incursions by the Israeli military into Palestinian refugee centers. Someone—Singleton?—had scrawled in bold black Magic Marker the single word: *WHY?* Nearby, Singleton had tacked an article about his brother and Loon Lake Ventures, David Singleton's first financial success. The same Magic Marker had written here: *LIES*.

Another panel contained a printout of a hundred or so names. Teachers, labor leaders, doctors, nurses. All with detailed identifying information, the kind Walker knew was usually available only to government agencies. Again, the Magic Marker: *ORDINARY CITIZENS WHO OPPOSE ISRAELI AGGRESSION*. He ran his finger along a thread that began at the list of names and continued to another pushpin attached to what appeared to be a printout of a website. Walker saw that it was the home page of a research organization whose name was unfamiliar to him. The site archived articles and studies on a variety of subjects published by several right wing think-tanks.

From there, other thick ganglia of red fanned out in various directions to the websites of an additional half dozen organizations, including a white survivalist group in Michigan and a Los Angeles-based Jewish defense group known to have disrupted Arab-American forums on the Middle East. More red threads ran from each group back to the list of American citizens.

Walker returned to the original website. At the bottom of the page, he saw a list of financial donors. Among them, Allan had high-lighted a single name: THE HARRISON BLEDSOE FOUNDATION FOR SOCIAL RESEARCH. "Bingo," Walker whispered to himself.

Walker sat down on the bed. Allan Singleton appeared to have stumbled onto a research group supported by one of Bledsoe's foundations, which, among other things, collected data on private citizens. What did the group do with the information? Walker thought of the extremist anti-abortion organizations from an earlier decade that published the home addresses of pro-choice doctors. Medical clinics had been bombed, some doctors shot dead outside their homes. Had the so-called War on Terror so polarized people in this country that opponents of the government's policies now had to fear for their very safety? It hadn't appeared to have happened yet, but it might, Walker reasoned. Singleton seemed to believe it was already happening. Walker tapped his finger on the red threads running to the defense league and survivalist group. Someone or some group had taken Singleton's poking around seriously; his research had clearly stirred up trouble for him. No wonder he'd decided to pull the plug on his former life and become Ollie Drupt. The man's apparent craziness was beginning to make sense.

Not only was it making sense, Walker realized, but these disquieting revelations raised a whole new set of questions. If some shadowy group, or even an intelligence agency, were looking for Allan, Quint must have been hired to get the disk for them or for somebody. Quint probably followed Walker, believing he would lead him to Singleton, and then when Walker learned where Allan lived, moved in and tried to take Allan's disc by force. Given the man's style and hair-trigger temperament, Walker could easily see him roughing up Singleton. Allan might have panicked and killed the detective in some kind of reflexive spasm of fear or self-defense. Walker knew that he had to be careful not to romanticize someone who so clearly demonstrated mental instability. Nevertheless, a new image of Singleton began to form inside Walker's head. Instead of an irrational killer with a grudge against authority figures, Singleton might really be a kind of *idiot savant* on a mission to warn people of danger. And his choice to confront Bledsoe in a public place surrounded by media and heavy security suggested Singleton was more concerned about getting his message out than visiting harm on Bledsoe as an individual.

Walker looked at his watch. It was early afternoon. He needed to set up across the street and wait for Singleton. Maybe Walker could talk Singleton out of showing up at a site where he would surely be arrested and instead offer him some alternatives. He could give him the name of an investigative reporter he knew, or get Delucca or another lawyer to sort out whatever criminal charges might be brought against him. He realized he had just accepted a new task: to protect Allan Singleton from the dangerous public image the man himself had created. Walker hoped that it was not too late.

Allan would have to come back for his suitcase and the portfolio. Walker decided to wait for him.

CHAPTER FOURTEEN

Summer fog encased Market Street, smudging streetlights and muffling the sounds coming from what little traffic still moved at this late hour. Metal awnings on shuttered bargain stores rattled and shook in the strong wind. A few hard core junkies were on the sidewalk, jittery hours away from their next fix, along with others with no other place to go, the desperate, the hungry, and the broken down. Like a brightly-lit cruise ship run aground on some remote shore, the marquee lights of the Cinema blazed in the middle of the block.

Across the street, a burly man wearing an Army jacket stood in a bus shelter, attempting to avoid the burger wrappers and newspapers eddying at his feet. With the practiced touch of a neurosurgeon, he plucked away a wrapper that had fastened itself to his baggy plaid pants. The man removed the floppy beret perched on his head and replaced it with an oversized Russian fur cap, which he pulled down hard over his forehead. His eyes never left the entrance to the Cinema.

McDonald's had long been closed for the day, but the bus kiosk provided him with a good view of the entrance without being seen himself. As customers filtered out of the Cinema, someone began to shutter the glass-encased poster displays flanking the entrance. Dancers in street clothes, a few carrying shapeless gym bags, came out singly or in pairs. The man shifted his feet, waiting. An empty blue, red and white Luxor cab rolled up and parked, its motor running. The man tensed—a radio dispatched call, he thought. An Asian-looking dancer in a red oil-skin raincoat ran out and got in the cab. The man relaxed.

Michaela emerged from the theatre and walked to the corner. He let her turn left on Seventh Street before he crossed Market, making *sure there was at least a block between them. She passed the Happy Daze Bar, the light from its open door momentarily illuminating her face. She looked tired, wan. At Stevenson Alley, she turned left again. Hurrying to keep up, he entered the mouth of the alley, no longer trying to keep out of sight. The alley was long and narrow and consisted of loading docks and service entrances for the Market Street stores. At this time of night, it was unpopulated and barren.*

Michaela had parked her car in the middle of the alley. As always, she checked for stalkers as she made her way to the car—girls from the Cinema had been accosted here before. Nothing. Except a homeless person in a ratty-looking fur hat and baggy pants shuffling in her direction. The man paused to peer into a dumpster. Michaela turned back and continued toward the car.

As soon as the woman turned, he picked up his pace, long strides now, the distance closing quickly between them. Michaela was reaching for the door handle when the first blow struck, staggering her to the ground onto her hands and knees. She realized something or someone had hit her on the back of the neck, and as she turned to look up, a knee smashed into her jaw. Strangely, Michaela felt numbness instead of pain. Floating on the edge of consciousness, she wondered if this is what it felt like to be dead, to be nothing. She became aware of hands moving up and down her body. The hands squeezed, patted, and tore at her clothing. She realized she was being searched. Then she sank into complete and total blackness.

CHAPTER FIFTEEN

The man known as Ollie Drupt left the bus at the corner of Old Bayshore and Geneva and began to trudge slowly towards the motel. It was nearly one o'clock in the morning and with his cardboard suitcase swinging from his tired arm, he could have been an office supply salesman returning from a long and not particularly successful road trip. Allan Singleton smiled to himself. One side of the street was in Daly City, the other in San Francisco. He was truly living on the edge.

At first, the little sports car parked across from the motel didn't seem out of place. The neighborhood was full of swap meets and flea markets where people bought and sold exotic items, including foreign car parts. Maybe the car was for sale, or perhaps its owner beached it at the curb to wait for some new part. He was a block away when he saw what he took to be some kind of movement in the rear plastic window. The door on the driver's side opened a few inches and a hand carefully set a cardboard coffee container on the pavement. A sharp gust of wind toppled the container and with a rattling sound, it rolled under the car. Singleton saw the door swing shut.

Ever since he had found the Bledsoe-supported web page, he feared he'd left some tell-tale electronic footprint for them to track. In the beginning, there were the seemingly innocuous email solicitations to join strange and unknown groups. The solicitations were soon followed by late night phone calls and hang-ups. That was when he left Berkeley for San Francisco and the anonymity of the city. Of course, like everything else in this life, the move was temporary. Finally, when they sent that man to Crystal's room, he knew he had to move again.

He would not give the person in the little sports car, whoever he was, the opportunity to capture him. The day after tomorrow was too important. Bledsoe and the people he wittingly or unwittingly supported had to be exposed. He would speak Truth to Evil.

The man known as Ollie Drupt casually bent to tie his shoe. He knew he could stay out of sight for the rest of the night. The fence around the power station was low enough he could climb over and sleep a few hours. In the morning, he would go downtown, find a Market Street movie house, and spend the day in the cool darkness. Afterwards, when it was dark again, finding a S.R.O. room for one night on Howard or Folsom Street would be relatively easy. He hated the idea of losing the display case, and all the work it represented. And the little computer. He opened his suitcase a couple of inches, saw that he had enough spare clothes, and reaching deeper under the lid, made sure that a packet of narrow red cylinders was still safe. Then, he clicked the lid closed, straightened up, and headed towards the power station.

By ten o'clock in the morning, Walker knew something was wrong. He got out of the MG, stretched his back, and headed towards the corner, his legs tingling and stiff from lack of movement. He turned the corner, backtracked to the motel, and went up to Singleton's rear window. It was not completely closed and Walker saw fingerprint smudges on the frame. He peered into the room. The computer and display were gone. Walker cursed and loped on wobbly legs back to his car.

Without the portfolio he had no way to prove what Allan was really up to. Walker thought of the disc. If he could get to Toby Wolfson in time for him to decipher it before Bledsoe's speech, maybe Singleton, with his power and connections, could convince Bledsoe's security people to put up their swords. He turned the ignition key and the engine caught.

A canary yellow late model Crown Victoria gunned its motor and slid   broadside across the sidewalk, slamming to a juddering stop ten feet from the front grill of the MG. Doors splayed open and suddenly two bulky men were closing on him fast. A meaty fist yanked Walker from the car onto his knees on the sidewalk. The smaller one had a dark automatic in his fist pointed at the middle of Walker's stomach. Walker's vision swam and he felt a sudden leaching of strength from his legs.

They moved in, one on each side of him.

"Pat him down, Lynch."

The man called Lynch was shorter by three inches than the other man and wore a tan windbreaker, black jeans and running shoes. Although he looked to be about the same age, his temples were streaked with gray. An Oakland Raiders cap, the bill squeezed like a baseball player's, rode uneasily on his round skull.

Lynch spun Walker around.

"Just to be sure. Hands on the hood. You know the drill."

Walker felt hands patting him down expertly.

"Inspector Gadget here is clean, Marty."

"A hundred and fifty applications for carry permits a year and only six granted, he doesn't want to be busted for not having the right paper."

Walker looked closely at the one called Marty. *Martin Caraway*, Walker thought. He recognized Caraway as one of several police officers charged with use of excessive force after raiding a gay rights fundraising party at a warehouse south of Market. Walker had worked on the case and his investigation had led to Caraway's reprimand and suspension.

Aware of adrenalin moving like a river in his nervous system, Walker fought to remain calm. He knew Caraway must remember him.

"Into the car, Walker. We're going to the Hall," Caraway said in a flat voice.

"For what?"

"Questioning."

Lynch opened the back door. Caraway placed his hand firmly on the top of Walker's head.

"Watch your noggin."

The pressure drove Walker back and down into the seat. The door clicked shut.

Ten minutes later, the Crown Vic shot down the ramp to the basement of the Hall of Justice. Walker had a fleeting out-of-body experience in which he seemed to float above scores of marked and unmarked vehicles in the garage. The car nosed to a stop next to a loading dock and like a shock cut in a movie, Walker was once more inside in the Crown Vic, looking towards the front seat and the side of Caraway's head. He noticed a small spot of jaw-line stubble Caraway must have missed during his morning shave.

Walker fought to focus, to concentrate on what was happening to him. His next perception was of being led into the homicide office, past a receptionist and toward a row of metal desks set against a wall. Lynch unclicked the handcuffs and told Walker to sit at one of the desks. The detectives moved a few steps away, talking in low voices. Walker strained but was unable to hear anything beyond the sibilant murmur of Lynch's voice punctuated by louder but unintelligible words from Caraway.

Walker glanced up at a bulletin board covered with notices: softball league schedules, potlucks, and a printed birth announcement. *"John and Lisa Rivera gave birth to a 5 lb 6 oz. baby girl on Saturday. Everyone is doing fine."* Underneath someone had scrawled: *"Even John?"*

The detectives came back to Walker's desk. Lynch sat down across from him, Caraway leaned against the wall. Lynch took off his cap and ran his fingers through his thinning hair and sighed.

"I wish I had your job, Walker. Chasing ambulances, delivering subpoenas."

"Sitting in your car, peeing in a bottle." This was from Caraway. "Good life you have there, Walker. Calm, uneventful."

"Sometimes not, though," Lynch interjected.

"I bet he likes it that way. I know I would." Caraway spread out his hands, turned them over. He appeared to be checking his nails.

"Been to the Hotel Seneca lately?" Lynch was looking directly into Walker's eyes.

Walker felt his gut tighten.

"Well, one of your persuasion, a private eye type, got himself whacked there this week. Know anything about it?"

"Is there a reason I should?"

"Frank A. Quint was the name of this unfortunate gumshoe. Frank *Augustus* Quint. Heard of him?"

"Never had the pleasure," Walker responded.

"He seemed to know you," Caraway went on. "We get a court order to go into his place and we find a shitload of notebooks listing a bunch of places where you've come and gone, complete with the hours, dates, and times. Looks like he was real interested in you."

"Maybe you got tired of this guy hounding you," Lynch said, pleasantly. "Maybe you decided to throw a scare into him. Pulled a piece on him, it went off somehow. Hell, I could understand that."

"An accident maybe. At worst, manslaughter," Caraway chimed in. "A jury might buy that, you never know."

Walker straightened his back. He had a hard time knowing which detective to watch. As he swung his eyes from one man to the other he found himself on the threshold of nausea.

"Look," he began. "I work a lot of cases. Civil and criminal. It wouldn't be all that unusual for somebody on the other side of a case to want to know what I'm up to. But to think I'd take out the guy who was watching me is ridiculous."

"Come on, Walker," Caraway said. "We got two witnesses that place you in the room. The deskman picked out your DMV picture. The guy's wife says you broke the news that her husband was dead."

"We could charge you right now," Lynch said in a calm, off hand manner. "You fit the frame very nicely indeed."

"Who's your client in this, Walker?" Caraway now, no pleasantness in his voice.

Walker sighed. "I can't give that up without their permission. You know that."

"Thought you might say something like that," Lynch answered, getting up. "Okay, I think we'll go on up to the seventh floor and leave you in a cell a while. You can think there."

"I want my phone call," Walker said evenly.

"You'll get it."

Walker held out his hands and felt the cool embrace of metal on his wrists.

CHAPTER SIXTEEN

Walker was taken to the seventh floor where he was printed, photographed, and issued an orange jump suit and a gray blanket. He watched as a clerk filled out an intake form. By craning his neck, Walker was able to read upside down in the space marked "charges" the words *Material Witness*. A sheriff's deputy with an aquiline nose and a stud earring, with whom Walker had a casual, nodding relationship, looked at him, raising one eyebrow in what was almost a stage gesture.

Two deputies he did not know led him into the Felony Wing. Neither man spoke. Walker became aware of several small mirrors poked from between cell bars checking him out as entered the row.

For a moment, Walker wondered if he would be put in protective custody or administrative segregation—special jail housing for prisoners who might be targeted by other inmates for reasons ranging from gang affiliation to the knowledge that they were informers. This treatment was also a courtesy frequently extended to "dirty" cops. Walker remembered waiting to meet a client for what, on paper at least, appeared to be a routine probation violation until he saw the inmate brought into the interview room shackled hand and feet. His client revealed that he'd been a San Quentin guard before a heavy drug habit drove him into street crime. If his former occupation were known to other prisoners, his life would be immediately at risk. Placing him in shackles was a kind of mime show, an attempt to make him look like a dangerous felon. Since private eyes occupied a shadowy gray area as far as law enforcement was concerned, Walker was reasonably certain that no one was going to offer him this courtesy. *Run Silent, Run Deep.* He would be an ordinary seaman on this voyage.

When he made his one phone call at the booking desk, Delucca told him they could not hold him longer than forty-eight hours without filing some kind of criminal charge.

"Listen, Malcolm. I want you to call someone at the Fairmont for me."

Walker instructed the attorney to tell David Singleton he had developed a lead on his brother.

"Tell him also that I have some important physical evidence. I need to get it to him ASAP."

"Assuming they cut you loose." The attorney's tone was cool and distant.

"Malcolm?"

"What?"

"It's me, Walker. Your old poker playing buddy, remember?"

"I'm half listening."

"I think Hassan Bakkrat is on the verge of breaking."

"For your sake, I hope he is."

Walker lay flat on his back on a hard bunk, hands clasped behind his head trying to shut out the unending noise, to flatten it somehow and make it dissolve across the audible spectrum. He viewed the task almost as a Zen exercise, designed to empty his mind of the sharp yells and percussive sounds of metal on metal, letting them fall away into a single musical note. In the end, he only succeeded in achieving a continuous ringing in his ears.

He thought of the time more than a quarter century ago when he had spent three nights in the New York City jail known as "The Tombs," arrested along with two dozen others in a sweep of an anti-war demonstration in Times Square. There had been noise then, too, but it had come from Walker's fellow prisoners as they sang songs most of the night. Walker recalled that repertoire included the Stones' "Satisfaction," as well as traditional civil rights and union songs.

He became aware of a cart creaking down the row toward him. An elderly black prisoner, reed-thin, hair white as cotton candy, dispensed Kool-Aid and peanut butter and jelly sandwiches. Walker greedily bit into the sandwich and was vaulted back in time to a summer camp many years ago in Maine, rain drumming on his poncho and those of his fellow cabin mates as they huddled together under tall pines in a torrential July downpour. The Kool-Aid, however, triggered no distant resonance—it merely tasted like what it was: tepid liquid Jell-O.

Walker slept erratically for unknown and unknowable chunks of time. He would doze off and then come suddenly awake, immediately aware of where he was and what had happened to him. His dreams were vivid, short, and frightening. In the first dream, he found himself underwater in a giant aquarium wrestling with a huge blue shark. The scene dissolved to the laconic face of Lynch standing outside Walker's cell as he pushed a photograph through the bars toward him. Walker looked at the photograph and saw Michaela's face, mottled and swollen. Lynch asked if he knew anything about it, since Walker's name had been found on a scrap of paper among her things. Lynch's face gave way to a bleak landscape in what Walker guessed was a rubble-strewn village somewhere in the Middle East. A boy in a bulky jacket walked up to Walker and smiled. Walker saw that it was Ali Bakkrat. The boy reached under his jacket for a detonating cord. In the instant before the flash of the explosion, the boy's face morphed into the features of Allan Singleton.

A shaken Walker woke to see the photograph lying next to his pillow and knew that Lynch had been there. The stark image of Michaela's disfigurement and pain burned into Walker's brain. He feared he was responsible for putting this already vulnerable woman at risk. This unspeakable, brutal attack on Michaela had to be linked to her retrieval of Allan's disc. Clearly, someone wanted it very badly. Perhaps one of the shadowy groups Allan had stumbled across. On the other hand, he would certainly want the disk back himself and therefore Allan could not be excluded as the perpetrator. Or the assault on Michaela could be completely unrelated, a grim spillover from her demimonde world of drugs and freelance espionage. If she weren't already on the run, Walker would have to get the answers from her. He rolled over and waited for sleep to wash over him again. After a great while, it finally came.

The next morning, after a march to the communal showers, Walker was back in his cell for an hour before he was called to an interview room. A tall young female assistant D.A. in her late twenties at the most told him he was free to go, but admonished him not to leave town without notifying her. He was to consider himself a potential witness until told otherwise. Walker responded that he always thought of himself as a witness—he was, after all, a professional observer. The woman did not smile.

It was noon by the time Walker was processed and released. Although he was freshly showered, his clothes seemed to stick to his skin and he was anxious to get home. He managed to flag down a cab and a quarter of an hour later stood in front of his front door searching for his keys. The door was unlocked. Walker nudged it open and took a step inside. Rooted to the floor, unable to take another step, Walker stared at his upturned desk, its drawers tilted at crazy angles, a snow storm of paper dusting the rug. Willing himself to move, he went quickly to the Venetian blinds and opened them. As he came back from the window, he saw Archie's bowl lying on its side on the floor. The small blue fish was on his belly in an inch of water, his gills moving spasmodically. Walker scooped up the bowl and went to the sink. Filling it with lukewarm water, he stuck his hand blindly into the kitchen cabinet, poked around for a moment, and came out with a small plastic bottle. He carefully squeezed three drops of anti-chlorine solution into the bowl. When he was finished, he carried it back to the windowsill.

Walker found and tipped upright his favorite chair and sank into it. Archie seemed to have recovered from his trauma. As if suddenly transported to a new world that demanded immediate exploration, the little fish was gliding and darting around the perimeter of his bowl. Walker's eyes panned the room. Television, computer, stereo all here. Not a robbery, clearly. The police? Walker did not put it past some elements in the department—Caraway seemed to be the kind of cowboy who might delight in this kind of search and destroy mission— but as follow-up intimidation to the message of a night in jail it was overkill and made little sense. If they wanted to toss his apartment to see what they could uncover, it would have been no problem to find some pliant judge who would sign a search warrant. Walker got up and, grunting, maneuvered his desk upright. He put the bulletin board back on its hook, pausing to look at Allan Singleton's computer-enhanced picture. Walker found his cordless phone under a pile of books and dialed Toby Wolfson's office at the Cal mathematics department. A recorded message informed him that Wolfson would return the following morning. Walker found Wolfson's home number through directory assistance and called it. Another answering machine. Same message. "Damn," Walker cursed under his breath.

Walker punched in the number for David Singleton's back line.

"Mr. Singleton, this is Walker."

"I've been waiting to hear from you." The voice was excited, on edge. "Where the hell have you been?"

"I'm sorry. I spent the night in jail."

Walker told Singleton about his night at the Hall and being out of phone contact.

"It's getting close, Walker. Tomorrow is Bledsoe's speech."

"Yes." A kind of bone weariness washed over him. He pinched the bridge of his nose and shook his head. "I know."

"I've alerted Bledsoe's security people and they are going to distribute Allan's picture."

"Listen to me very carefully." Walker resumed his neatening and straightening. "They need to stand down."

"I don't understand."

"I don't think Allan is dangerous. I mean, we can't say conclusively that he is a threat." *Careful, Walker. You have no proof either way. You're skating on thin ice.*

"Well, this certainly changes things."

"I found something that should confirm what I'm telling you."

"Great."

Walker opened his front door and went into the hallway, where he carefully removed a sconce from a Deco light fixture.

"It's a computer disc that belonged to Allan."

Walker retrieved an oilskin pouch taped to the wall. He opened it and pulled out the disc.

"Do you know what's on it?"

"Not yet. But I think it's the reason Quint was killed."

"Can you bring it to me tonight?"

"I won't know what's on it until tomorrow."

"All right. Bring it then."

"You'll be there?"

"Of course. I want to make sure that those goons treat Allan properly if he does show up. He's still my brother, after all."

"All right. I'll get there as early as I can."

"Nice going, Walker. See you tomorrow."

Walker hung up and went about restoring his apartment to some minimum version of livability. What was irretrievably broken went into a trash bag; salvageable papers and files were scooped into piles to be sorted through later. The work was slow and hard, but Walker finished it by mid-afternoon. As far as he could tell, nothing was missing. Several times, Walker had picked up the phone and called the Cinema to leave messages for Michaela. She had not called back.

Walker fed Archie from his stash of dried bloodworms, the little fish's special treat food. He turned on the stove and selected a Lean Cuisine Salisbury steak from the freezer. He nuked it in the microwave, and ate it by the window as he watched a pewter-colored sky turn dark purple. He turned his head at a soft rustling sound at his door.

Walker stood at the door listening, his Detective Special held loosely at his thigh. When he heard no more sounds, he yanked open the door and stepped quickly to the side.

Michaela's eyes went wide and she moved back, bringing her forearm protectively to her face.

"God, Walker," she said, her eyes on the gun.

"Come inside."

Walker put the gun in his waistband and led her by the elbow to the couch. Michaela winced as he snapped on a table lamp. Her deep bruises—one as big as a pancake spreading from the point of her jaw to her right upper cheekbone—appeared worse than what he had seen in the photograph.

Walker got out a three-year old bottle of Chilean Merlot and went to work with a corkscrew.

"Tell me what happened."

"It was in the alley after work," Michaela responded, accepting a brimming glass. "The man looked like he was a homeless person. At first I thought it was a robbery, but he never went for my purse."

"Did you see his face?"

"I don't know. It all happened so fast."

Walker returned to the desk, found the picture of Allan Singleton and brought it over to Michaela. After studying it for a long moment, Michaela sighed.

"There is a resemblance. The eyes. It could be." She sighed again. "I don't know, Walker."

"Shit."

"I'm sorry."

"No, I didn't mean that."

"You don't want it to be him, do you?"

"I guess I don't."

Walker went over and fed Archie some more bloodworms.

"I meant I was sorry that I involved you in this."

"I was already involved." Michaela said quietly.

Walker turned back from the bowl, looking at her now.

"The people I work for, I guess you could call them my handlers..."

"Call them whatever you want."

"Last month they asked me to watch him."

"Who?"

"The man in the picture."

Walker picked up the picture again and held it up.

"Allan Singleton?"

Michaela nodded.

"Did you?"

"Did I what?"

"Watch him."

"No. I said I would, but I lied to them. As I told you, by then it all had become just so much make-believe for me."

"They tell you why they were interested in him?"

"They said something about his being some kind of radical, hippy mathematics person."

"But why this particular guy?"

"They claimed he was a threat to national security. Apparently he had been able to break into a sensitive and classified website. So when Crystal told me about the disc, I thought it might have something to do with that."

Walker thought of the list of citizen names.

"What we saw on the disc certainly looks a lot more like equations and formulas."

"He's a mathematician, Walker," Michaela answered. "It could be his way of encrypting and protecting it."

Walker was silent for a moment.

"When you said you knew somebody who could decipher the disc, you meant your friends at the Consulate?"

"Please believe me, Walker. I am through with those people. I wanted to give it to a local human rights group."

Walker wished he could get the disc to Wolfson tonight. Tomorrow would have to do.

"What about Crystal?"

"What about her?"

"I never totally bought the idea that a stripper her age would hang out with a middle-aged, socially maladroit guy like Allan."

"I don't know. A father figure maybe? Crystal said he used to take her to dinner and she'd tell him about a five hundred dollar Hermes scarf she saw at Neiman Marcus. A week later, he'd show up with a hundred dollar knock-off that he'd found somewhere on Stockton Street in Chinatown. She thought it was sweet and never called him on it."

"Doesn't matter. Somebody still could've paid Crystal to get close to Allan."

"You certainly have a cynical view of human nature, Walker."

"Perhaps."

Walker got up and strode to the window. In the distance, he saw a large sailing schooner glide toward Alcatraz Island, resembling some phantom ship from the past.

"You probably want to know why you should believe any of this."

Walker looked back from the window, the beginnings of a wry smile on his face.

"The thought occurred to me."

"Well, maybe you will if I give you something you told me you wanted."

"I don't know what the hell you're talking about."

"Ahmed Bakkrat."

"Ahmed Bakkrat?"

"Yes. The brother of the man you were writing that report about."

"Yes. I remember. You called him a famous martyr."

Michaela paused and looked up at Walker. Her eyes were clear and steady.

"I saw a transcript of their interrogation of Hassan Bakkrat."

"They interrogated *Hassan*?"

"Yes. It was considered a model interrogation. Some of it was excerpted in a training manual. That's how I saw it."

"Go on."

"The army wanted Ahmed. He was the political one. They reasoned that the way to him was through Bakkrat. The interrogation sessions—and I can assure you there was more than one session—progressed in stages beginning with sleep depravation, moving on to loud noises and constant light, and finally, dogs were introduced. Barking, snapping dogs. There was more, but those pages were blacked out."

Walker did not answer. Muscles in his jaw worked convulsively. His eyes fought to focus the small human shapes performing unseen tasks on the schooner's main deck.

"Eventually, his skilled interrogators got what they wanted: the brother's daily route to work. A week later they blew him up, Walker. He had stopped at a red light in Gaza City, a helicopter appeared suddenly over the roof line, a rocket flew straight into his car. Blew him to kingdom come."

Walker watched the schooner disappear behind Alcatraz.

"The disc may prove whether I am telling the truth or not. Let me take it to my friend."

"I can't do that, Michaela." Everybody, including David Singleton, suddenly seemed to want the disc.

"Why not?"

"One person has already been killed because of this damn disc. A poor dumb private eye like me."

"He could've been working for Israeli Intelligence, for God's sake. They use all kinds of people." Michaela's smile was bitter at its edges.

"Why didn't you quit—just walk away?"

"They said if I did they would see that my drug use came out—I would be deported and never work in Israel again."

Walker moved to the couch and sat down next to Michaela.

"All I know is that nobody's getting the disc until I get it deciphered."

"And how is that going to happen?"

"I'm going to show it to a colleague of Allan's at U.C. Berkeley first thing in the morning."

"Can I come with you?"

"There's not a whole lot of time."

Michaela drew in her breath and sighed.

"Okay, perhaps after he deciphers it," Walker responded.

"Thank you, Walker," Michaela smiled. "I suppose that indicates a certain level of trust."

"A certain level, yes." Walker smiled back.

Michaela leaned over and kissed Walker on the forehead and got up. She went to the sink and rinsed out her glass. She stood next to Walker's desk, nervously fingering some loose papers.

"I only came tonight because I knew you'd be worried if I didn't." She looked down absently at articles Walker had copied about David Singleton's business empire.

Words came to Walker, but he could not find their right order and chose to say nothing.

"I'm going home, Walker," Michaela continued. "To the Middle East. My brother has a place in Lebanon."

"If you need anything, anything at all—"

"There's nothing. Thank you."

Michaela moved to Walker's desk and scribbled something on a piece of paper.

"My email address."

She placed it on the desk. Her eyes moved to an article from a business journal showing a picture of David Singleton.

"I don't know what is real or what is not anymore."

"Join the club." Walker poured himself some more Merlot.

"For example, this picture," Michaela continued. She held it up so Walker could see. "This man also looks like the person who attacked me."

"That's because he's Allan's brother."

"I am unable to choose between them. For me, they are the same person."

"Very existential, Michaela." Walker smiled.

"Perhaps." She moved toward him. Walker rose and embraced her. Michaela rested her head on his shoulder for a long moment. Then she turned toward the door.

"You're not so bad, Walker," she smiled. "But you're in over your head."

In a moment, she was gone. Walker went around the apartment turning off lights. He did not undress. He lay on the couch and thought about what Michaela had revealed about Hassan Bakkrat. Why had he given up his own brother to Israeli security forces and certain death? Was there more? Walker's life seemed to be cluttered with pairs of troubled and troubling brothers. But before there could be answers, Walker knew he first must save a life tomorrow.

CHAPTER SEVENTEEN

Walker's MG ground steadily up the long incline of the Bay Bridge leading to the Treasure Island tunnel and home. Directly ahead in the distance, San Francisco seemed to float on water. The sports car punched through the dark circle of the tunnel onto the suspension section of the bridge and the sudden surge of sunlight created the momentary illusion of the entire city dancing for a few seconds on the nose of the vibrating hood. After a few hours of fitful sleep, Walker had arisen, made some coffee and toast, and waited for morning. When dawn finally creased the eastern sky with pink streaks of light, he left the apartment and drove in light traffic across the Bay Bridge to Berkeley. He killed another hour drinking coffee at an outdoor kiosk while he waited for the Math Department office to open.

Walker entered the building at a few minutes after nine and nearly panicked when Wolfson was not in his office. The departmental secretary informed him that the professor was teaching a seminar down the hall. Walker found the classroom and peered through a window in the door. Inside, Wolfson spoke to a cluster of grad students seated in an informal arc in front of him. One of the students pointed at Walker and Wolfson came over to open the door.

"Sam Spade. Find your man yet?"

"Almost, but not quite," Walker replied, removing the disc from his pocket. "I need you to take a look at this."

Wolfson took the disc and glanced inquiringly at Walker.

"What is it?"

"Something that might prove Allan Singleton is not a threat to anyone."

"I can't get to it until tonight or tomorrow morning—is that all right?"

"I really need it yesterday."

"Tell you what." Wolfson walked over to a desk and slid the disc into a computer. "I'll make a copy to analyze and you keep the original."

Walker heard whirring and clunks and a moment later Wolfson handed the disc to Walker, who thanked him and backed out of the classroom.

As he downshifted from fourth to third gear to begin the gentle descent into San Francisco, Walker felt the tug of David Singleton's disc against the material of his shirt pocket. He checked his watch—the speech would not start for another forty minutes.

Walker eased the MG into the far right lane and slowed as the bridge deck dipped toward the San Francisco anchorage. He took the Fremont Street exit and headed for the northern waterfront and the plaza where Bledsoe was scheduled to speak.

The landscaped isosceles triangle at the base of Telegraph Hill featured a perpetual waterfall built from slabs of quarried rock set in a gently rolling lawn. Sandblasted brick shops and stores occupied former warehouses, packinghouses, and chandleries that at one time had served a thriving Embarcadero waterfront. Walker circumnavigated the plaza's perimeter, first driving north on Sansome Street and then swinging back south on Battery where a small crowd of perhaps seventy-five people clustered near a raised podium at the end of the plaza. Walker noticed a handful of men in dark suits, still as weather vanes on a calm day, spaced at irregular intervals along the sidewalk. Several uniformed police officers were also present. David Singleton was nowhere in sight.

Walker left his car in the only public garage in the vicinity and glanced at his ticket: charges were imposed every twenty minutes. He ducked into a shop that advertised itself as a French bakery and bought an overpriced container of coffee, that he took out to the sidewalk to drink. Once more he took in the scene. No one seemed out of place, a player in a different movie.

He went up to one of the dark suits and asked to speak to a supervisor. Walker was directed to a tall fiftyish man with close-cropped iron-gray hair. Like the other suits, he wore an earpiece with a filament-thin wire that snaked inside his lapel. Walker showed him his P.I. license. The man introduced himself as Bill Mahoney, Bledsoe's security chief. Walker asked him if he had seen David Singleton.

"Not yet. He should be here. Don't worry, he got the picture to us. We're set."

"Look, there's been a change. I have new information."

Mahoney looked closely at Walker.

"What kind of information?"

Walker began to explain that Allan was an idiosyncratic whistle blower, not a lone terrorist. A single helicopter chattered overhead. Mahoney angrily jabbed his finger toward the sky—Walker recognized the call letters of a local TV station on the side of the mechanical bird—and spoke rapidly into his lapel mike. A few moments later, the helicopter disappeared over the crest of Telegraph Hill. When the sound subsided and Mahoney looked back at Walker, his eyes were distant and cool.

Something definitely was not right. The whole security arrangement reeked of overkill. *Where the hell was David Singleton?*

"You really need to back off some of your men," Walker pressed ahead. "The only danger Allan Singleton poses right now is to himself."

"That's not the message I got from your client last night. He told me that Allan Singleton was at the University of Wisconsin when that building went up and a graduate student got killed."

"He told you that *last* night?"

"Made a point of it."

"That's fucked up. Something is very wrong here."

"Hey, I can't have my men stand down on your word alone."

Walker followed Mahoney's gaze towards several men at the periphery of the crowd. He thought he could make out lightweight but deadly machine pistols beneath their bulky ski parkas.

"I can straighten this out when Singleton gets here." His eyes swept the plaza again for his client. The crowd seemed composed for the most part of office workers and a few retirees—one part of Walker's brain wondered how much compensation they received from Bledsoe for sacrificing their lunch hours to listen to their boss.

Walker moved quickly away from Mahoney and scoured the plaza again. He paused for a moment to look up at the craggy, rock-strewn face of Telegraph Hill rising steeply from the street. Some loose shale from the cliff lay at the edge of the sidewalk. Walker bent over to pick up a small piece. It crumbled in his hand. A strong wind coming off the Embarcadero shifted some of the shards in his palm. Walker looked up and saw several SFPD marksmen poised on the lip of the cliff. Walker knew he had to find Allan before he was captured. Or worse.

Most of the sparse crowd had settled expectantly into metal folding chairs in front of the podium when a latecomer, a pudgy, middle-aged man in a light windbreaker, squeezed into one of the last open chairs in the section. The plastic ID card on his jacket identified him as a Certified Vendor to the Bledsoe Family Foundation. It had not been hard to come by—two weeks earlier, pretending to be a software salesman, Allan Singleton had visited the Bledsoe world headquarters during an open house for software suppliers, and when he was sure no one was looking, simply pocketed a blank visitor's pass that he later filled out.

Harrison Bledsoe, dressed casually in a gray sports jacket, regimental striped tie and gray twill pants, strode to the platform. What appeared to be a year-round tan contrasted nicely with his smooth features and clear blue eyes. Allan noticed that Bledsoe's facial muscles were unnaturally tight and he speculated that extensive surgery accounted for Bledsoe's appearing ten years younger than the age his biographers accorded him. Bledsoe began to speak about volunteerism and the importance of preserving the ecosphere while renewing energy sources.

"Gibberish! This person speaks nothing but gibberish!"

The man in the windbreaker with the laminated ID badge stood up, pulled several typed manuscript pages from his pocket, and began to read in a loud, firm voice. The breeze coming off the water had picked up in intensity and Walker heard only a few disjointed phrases. A few words cut through: *"obscene profits...enemies lists...foundations with secret agendas."* Entire sentences were swept away in the wind.

Walker saw the laminated badge and immediately began pushing people and chairs out of his way as he fought through the crowd towards Singleton. Heads everywhere turned in Allan's direction. Bledsoe stopped speaking and stared at Allan, his mouth open in what was either a bemused smile or a gaping rictus of fear.

From the left side, two men in dark suits stepped forward. As if he had expected this, Allan Singleton turned to face the intruders. He unzipped his jacket and spread it open, revealing twin rows of cylinder-shaped red objects taped to his mid section. The two security men stopped in mid stride as if they were in a schoolyard game of musical chairs. Singleton smiled at them and continued to read. With each measured sentence, he took a step closer to Bledsoe, whose eyes were like saucers now.

Walker slowed to a walk as he came within ten feet of Singleton. Willing Allan to make eye contact, he spread his arms out, palms open, to show he was unarmed. In his peripheral vision, Walker saw Maloney grab the forearm of one of the security men and push him forward. Crouching, the man approached Singleton at an oblique angle, his eyes never leaving him. Walker veered to intercept the man. The security agent's coat came open and the snout of a Tech Nine machine pistol pointed at Walker. He froze and put up his hands.

The weapon swung toward Singleton and a wisp of gray smoke appeared, punctuated by sharp hammering pops. With a slight frown, Singleton turned toward the source of the shots, a puzzled expression on his face.

Walker ran toward Singleton, who seemed to sway like a sapling in a strong breeze. Rivulets of blood fanned out across Allan's forehead. For a single, crazed moment, Walker was reminded of Allan's collage, with its network of red thread. Singleton fell to his knees and pitched forward into Walker's arms.

For several long seconds, nobody moved. Bledsoe stared down from the podium, his face slack and haggard. Then, as if death was a contagion that could transfer to them, people scattered, fell, and stumbled away from Walker.

Walker lowered Singleton's motionless body to the grass, his forefinger on his neck, searching for a pulse. He gently turned the body over. Walker saw Mahoney's eyes widen and his mouth form the word *shit* as Walker removed one of the red cylinders. It was a highway flare.

"You shouldn't touch him," Mahoney said sharply.

"You shouldn't have shot him!" Walker shot back, his eyes stinging with tears.

Walker handed the flare to Mahoney and turned back to Singleton. Neither of the two age-enhanced photos had quite got it right. Singleton had aged according to his own private trajectory. The eyes were the unchanged constant, penetrating and deep even in death. Walker reached out and closed them. This time, Mahoney did not protest.

Walker straightened up and looked around.

A man was pushing a shopping cart down Sansome Street away from the podium. There was something familiar about the torn army jacket, the plaid slacks puddling at the man's ankles, and the black beret drawn low across the forehead. Walker moved toward the man, his hand inside his jacket, feeling for his gun. Instead, his fingers found the computer disc. The .38 Detective Special was under the front seat of his car.

Rattles and squeaks from the cart's worn wheels grew louder as Walker gained on it. He remembered the jacket and the beret from his confrontation with Quint near the Hall of Justice. This was one of the two men who had intervened to protect him from Quint. When he was three feet from the man's back, Walker reached out to grab him by the shoulder.

The man spun around and beneath the pulled-down beret and a three-day stubble of beard, a fierce smile burned like a blast furnace.

"Let's go somewhere and talk, Walker."

He continued to smile as he showed Walker a small silver automatic in his waistband.

CHAPTER EIGHTEEN

The man in the black beret tilted his head toward the cart, gesturing to Walker to keep in front of him as they moved away from the plaza. The cart creaked and rattled, and neither man spoke as the cluster of people around Allan Singleton's body receded in the distance. Walker made an attempt to catch Mahoney's eye, but the man kept his body and the cart between them, blocking Mahoney's line of sight.   When they reached the end of Sansome and crossed the Embarcadero, the man pointed to a break in a chain link fence leading out to a derelict wooden pier. He followed Walker onto the warped and bleached wooden planks, the little silver gun out in the open now, pointing at Walker's back. The man stopped, leaned against a creosote-streaked piling, and casually waved the gun at Walker, indicating that he should sit facing him.

With his free hand, the man removed his beret and carefully put on a pair of glasses. Sunlight glinted off a metal neck chain attached to the glasses as he removed his soiled leather jacket and placed it on the planking next to him.

"You have the disc, I assume," David Singleton asked.

"This whole thing is about the disc?"

"It's always been about the disc." Singleton leveled the gun at Walker's chest.

Walker stared hard at the face, with its brownish-yellow pancake make up. He looked away and down at the brackish water and found himself thinking about rivers, Mark Twain and friendly con artists and hucksters. And failed actors. The man sitting across from him was certainly all of these.

Walker reached in his pocket and came up with the disc. For a moment, he thought of letting it fall into the bay. As if he read Walker's thoughts, Singleton's free hand darted out and snatched it from him.

"Thank you."

Singleton dropped the disc into an inside pocket.

"Can we put the gun away now?"

"No," Singleton answered.

"You killed him."

"No, *they* killed him, Walker."

"With your help."

"The Allan I knew died a long time ago."

Walker shifted his position to lean against a thick wooden post. He smelled creosote and felt the old pier shift position as each wave gently slapped at the pilings below.

"My brother was blackmailing me. Shouldn't surprise you, Walker, being the man of the world that you are."

"Save it, Singleton. Tell me what the hell has been going on here."

Singleton looked back at the downtown skyline for a long moment as if the answer might reside in its tall buildings.

"My brother was always a problem. Going back to the fire at Loon Lake, which I'm sure you know about by now. I always protected him. From the beginning, the fire marshal's suspicions centered on Allan. He was the younger, angry brother. I was seen as the older, responsible sibling incapable of such an impulsive act. I tried to convince them of Allan's innocence but their suspicion continued to the point where Allan wasn't sure what happened himself."

"Did he set the fire?"

"No. They did. My parents were in the midst of one of their violent drunken arguments. Allan was asleep in his room. My father threatened to throw a kerosene lamp into my mother's face. She dared him to do it. I tried to intervene and the lamp went over. First her clothes caught fire. Then the floor. The house was built out of Adirondack pine and everything went up like a tinder box. I grabbed Allan from his room and ran to the lake."

"In the article I saw, you didn't tell the fire marshals any of this. Why not?"

"I tried. But they didn't listen. They said there was no forensic evidence."

"What did you tell Allan?"

"I told him it was an accident. That the wick in the lamp was faulty."

"Did he believe you?"

"At first he seemed to. But it was always there, submerged. It was as if that terrible night had driven a permanent wedge between us. We stopped talking. From a distance, I followed his career at Berkeley. He seemed to be doing well. Then he suddenly walked away from everything he'd achieved."

"Then the notes starting coming, almost daring you to find him."

"Yes."

"I didn't see all of them, did I? You held some back."

"My brother was blackmailing me, Walker."

Walker thought he heard the rise and fall of a siren in the distance. He wondered if it was the coroner's wagon coming for Allan Singleton.

"About Loon Lake?"

"He always suspected that I was involved. But what brought it to a head was the research he did on Bledsoe."

"I don't understand."

"When Allan was a graduate student, he developed a new kind of common programming language," Singleton continued. "Something to do with the mathematical concepts of class and sets. He sent me an article he published in a scholarly journal. I think he wanted his big brother to be proud of him. I was tired of sitting in cafes and my acting career was going nowhere, so I had an engineer friend look at the article. He immediately recognized the practical applications. With some tinkering and a few changes, they became the basis of my first start up company. Back in those days it was hard to lose money on anything related to computers. After a couple of years, I sold the company to Harrison Bledsoe for a lot of money. The program is now used in all his inventory tracking programs."

"You're talking about Loon Lake Ventures?"

Singleton nodded.

"Four months ago, I heard from Allan for the first time in years. He wrote to say that in the course of doing research on Bledsoe, he came across the original Loon Lake website. Allan immediately saw that it was based largely on his earlier work. He was outraged that his ideas were now linked to a person, to use his words, as monstrous as Bledsoe. He said he would let Silicon Valley and Wall Street know that that Bledsoe's success was in part based on ideas that had been ripped off from a graduate student. If I didn't blow the whistle on Bledsoe, he would publicly implicate me in our parents' deaths. Even though it was a bluff, pure fantasy lacking any supporting evidence, the publicity would not be good for me. Or for Bledsoe. I warned Bledsoe and together we decided we had to find Allan."

"So you hired me."

"Bledsoe knew your old college friend, Jacobson, from his athletic club. Jacobson told me you were a nice guy who was somewhat down on his luck, and well, it seemed like a good fit. We needed a generic gumshoe—to use a baseball analogy, a basic .218 utility infielder—because if someone with only moderate abilities could find him, then a lawyer, graduate student, journalist, FTC investigator, whatever, certainly would be able to turn him up."

"What about Quint? Was he part of your plan, too?

"Yes. I felt I needed someone to keep track of you."

"And the little charade outside the Hall of Justice?"

"Quint wanted a diversion so he could put a tracking device in the wheel well of your car."

Walker had a memory image of Quint kneeling next to the MG's front wheel and realized why he never saw the brown van on his tail.

"How did you find out about the disc?"

"Quint stumbled onto it. He followed you that day when you first went to that hotel. He came back later and overheard Allan talking to his girlfriend about a disc he wanted her to hold for him. Quint assumed that it must be valuable. You see, I'd already told him in general terms that Allan had something he could use to blackmail and Quint assumed the disc must be what I was talking about."

"His wife said he had a nose for money."

"Quint turned out to be a greedy hothead. He asked me to come to that girl, Crystal's, hotel room. When I got there, he tried to convince me that he had found the disc—I assumed of course that it must contain the equations and codes I'd borrowed from Allan to start Loon Lake. Quint demanded that I pay for the disc. One hundred thousand dollars, up front. He was waving this around..." Singleton lifted the small gun up from his lap. "I lost my head and struggled with him for it. The gun went off, shooting him in the chest. I panicked and rolled his body under the bed and left."

"You weren't so completely panicked that you didn't forget to search the room for the disc."

"Yes, of course, Walker. I felt I had a moral right to its contents. Without my giving Allan's ideas a practical application, they would have languished as an academic oddity, nothing more."

Walker looked intently at Singleton.

"That wasn't all, was it?"

"What do you mean?"

"Maybe Quint's death happened the way you said it happened, maybe it didn't," Walker continued. "We'll probably never know. But I'm sure you realized that once the police got to Crystal and heard her story, they would think that Allan shot Quint and you'd be off the hook."

"That only occurred to me later. At the time, I was too upset to think rationally."

"If the police take a close look, I doubt they'll buy your story, Singleton."

"Who are they going to believe—the allegations of a moderately successful gumshoe or the word of someone who is the president of three high-tech companies? Besides, you have no independent proof."

Singleton threw the leather jacket into the water. The beret followed.

"Then there is the issue of your character," Singleton continued. "I know from a friend on the police commission that at the moment you are viewed very skeptically in your profession. You are about a step away from losing your license."

"Don't count on it," Walker responded.

Singleton smiled.

"I like you, Walker. After all, you did get the disc for me. I can have a generous bonus delivered to you tomorrow morning."

"I'm not interested in your money, Singleton."

"As you wish."

Walker looked at Singleton.

"What happens next?"

Singleton seemed amused by the question.

"Nothing happens. Tomorrow, I step in as the grieving, caring brother and arrange Allan's funeral and memorial service. Next week, I begin a nine-week cruise of the Greek islands and you go about doing whatever it is a guy like you does after he has finished a case."

Singleton turned to go.

"Bullshit." Walker voice was tense, hard. "You're just a sadistic, greedy motherfucker. All the rest is bullshit."

Walker stood up and faced him

"I think you wanted your brother dead because he could implicate you in your parents' death. You always worried that maybe he wasn't really asleep when the house went up, but he had stayed quiet for years until your avarice stirred everything up. Then things quickly got out of hand. I think you hired Quint to kill your brother once I found him. The guy had just lost his license for crossing the line, he wasn't exactly savory, and he was just the kind of low-life who would do it for you."

Singleton took out his gun again and held it at his side, pointing it down at the deck.

"But Quint's death gave you another option," Walker went on. "You realized Allan would be a suspect. And if you couldn't frame your brother for Quint's death, you had yet another plan."

"I don't know what you're talking about."

"Yes, you do." Walker's voice was steady, uninflected.

He stood up and pushed Singleton's cart over the lip of the pier and into the water. Walker watched with satisfaction as it sunk to the bottom, leaving a thin stream of bubbles.

Singleton leveled the gun at Walker.

"It would be better if you sat down."

"Or you'll shoot me?" Walker shrugged. "I don't think so. You'd have a hard time explaining it."

"You're forgetting we are seventy-five yards from shore. The shot would just sound like a backfire from a motorboat."

Walker remained standing, his back against the pylon.

"If you couldn't frame your brother for the murder, you knew Bledsoe's people could take him out and, given the state of paranoia in the world today, no one would look too closely at the death of some half crazed, middle-aged hippy who threatened a respected captain of industry."

"I didn't want to see my brother killed, Walker."

"If they didn't follow your little scenario and kill him when he surfaced at Bledsoe's speech, you knew at the very least that he could be jailed for making threats to Bledsoe, which would buy you more time while you went after the disc."

Walker paused, watching Singleton's face.

"Allan didn't attack the girl from the Cinema in that alley," Walker went on. "It was you, looking for the disc, wasn't it?"

Singleton did not respond.

"Goddamn you for that," Walker said evenly.

Singleton turned his back on Walker and moved to the edge of the pier. After a moment, he turned around.

"No one is going to believe you, Walker. Certainly, you know that."

"There's something else you should know."

Singleton stopped and looked at Walker.

"What you think is on the disc may not be there," Walker said calmly.

"Nice try, Walker."

"Your brother was in possession of some very sensitive material an intelligence agency wanted back. That may be why, ultimately, he was gunned down. How does that grab you, Singleton?"

"You're full of shit." The gun swung towards the middle of Walker's chest. Singleton took a step closer to Walker.

"The other thing you should know is the disc you have is a copy," Walker continued, his words rushing and clumping together. "The original is being examined right now by one of your brother's former colleagues in Berkeley. He also has a note from me saying what he should do if I suddenly turn up missing."

"Cheap bluff." Singleton's face was flushed, contorted.

"I don't think you want to wait to find out," Walker said.

Singleton squeezed off a shot and Walker felt hot air rush by his temple. He took two long strides towards Singleton, pushed off and came up at him under the man's gun hand before Singleton could fire again. It was a football open field block, the kind Walker had often thrown many years ago in school, and it struck Singleton in his mid section, causing him to stagger backward to the lip of the pier. For a long moment, Singleton teetered on the edge in slow motion before he spun half-way around and fell backward into the bay. Walker heard a soft splash and moved quickly to the edge. Looking down, he saw Singleton's head bobbing in the water fifteen feet below, his arms windmilling. From what seemed like a great distance, Singleton's voice floated up to him: *"I can't swim!"*

Walker picked up Singleton's gun and put it in the pocket of his leather jacket. He bent over, removed his shoes, dropped the jacket on the planking and lifted off the dock in a smooth downward arc. The water came up fast, meeting his face with a cold slap. He entered a green, silent world, his momentum carrying him downward until he did a forward summersault and righted himself. Relaxing his body, he let his own buoyancy lift him back to the surface. The gentle swell made the horizon line tilt crazily. Walker saw Coit Tower and Telegraph Hill alternately rise and then fall beneath the water, only to reappear as if seen through a periscope. He bicycled his legs, churning and treading water to stay afloat, but he could not see Singleton.

More long seconds passed. Ten yards toward the shore, Singleton's head broke through the surface only to go under again a moment later. Walker turned his face into the water and began a fast overhand crawl toward the place where he had seen Singleton's head disappear. Walker's legs scissor-kicked as he worked to establish a consistent rhythm with his arm strokes. Once he reached what he guessed was the spot, he treaded water and waited for the head to reappear. When it did not, Walker bent over at the waist, and dove as deep as he could into the green darkness.

Walker saw Singleton ahead of him, sinking slowly, his arms held in close to his body, slowing twisting as he went down like a tango dancer without a partner. Walker swam closer, caught Singleton under the armpits and, kicking hard, brought him to the surface. Both men gasped and drank deep draughts of air. Suddenly, Walker felt Singleton's fingers encircle his neck in panic. As Walker fought to pry them loose, Singleton's greater weight dragged both of them beneath the surface.

Cold and numbing darkness surrounded Walker. His lungs burned and ached. Singleton's eyes were closed and air bubbles were leaking from the corner of his mouth. They continued to sink. The sensation of cold was replaced with a feeling of warmness and Walker felt a strange lassitude, an almost overwhelming weariness. He knew he must not let this man take him into complete darkness. Walker's legs begin to bicycle again. His left foot struck something. Both feet came to rest on a platform of some kind. It was Singleton's upturned shopping cart, resting on the muddy and debris-strewn bottom. Walker's muscular-skeletal system regrouped and he flexed into a compact crouch. Holding Singleton by the waist, he summoned all his energy and pushed off.

Several long seconds later, he broke the surface, his lungs on fire and his mouth tasting of oil slick. He shifted his grip on Singleton so that his right arm snaked across the man's chest and hooked around his back. Above him, Walker saw that it would be impossible to climb back up onto the pier—the distance from the water's surface to the top of the deck appeared to be at least ten feet and there were no hand holds visible. Looking back towards shore, Walker decided his best chance would be the point where the pier joined the Embarcadero—where people were. He began to stroke with his left arm towards the shore, now perhaps sixty yards away. Walker worked slowly and methodically, and yard-by-yard, he steadily gained ground. As he drew closer to land, Walker saw movement and shapes. The moving shapes became a small crowd. Minutes later, hands reached down for Singleton's limp body, lifting him up to the breakwater. Walker saw several firemen, Mahoney, and someone who looked like Lynch.

He was pulled out of the water by strong hands and wound up lying on his stomach, panting. He saw the face of Michael Botin smiling down at him, urging him to breathe. Two fireman performed CPR on Singleton, who appeared to not be responding. Walker closed his eyes and went to sleep.

CHAPTER NINETEEN

Walker's teeth chattered as he struggled to swallow the hot chicken broth being fed to him. His clothes had been removed and a heavy navy blue blanket hung like a tent on his shoulders, covering his nakedness. That part of his conscious mind still taking in sensory information told him he was in the white-tiled wardroom of the Harbor Fire Station. Outside the lead-framed window, he saw a million dollar view of Treasure Island and the Bay Bridge. In his present woozy state, Walker very much wanted to become a fireman, to move in with them immediately and become part of their world. He had always admired the way they navigated their universe of danger with a kind of light grace.

Walker's inchoate thoughts quickly dissolved as a black Raiders baseball cap filled his field of vision. Under the brim, Inspector Lynch's weathered face broke into something approaching a smile.

"I see you're back with us, Walker."

Walker tensed, not ready for a confrontation.

"I meant back with the living," Lynch went on, carefully easing his middle-aged bulk down on the wooden bench next to Walker. "They tell me you swallowed a lot of water."

Lynch looked at one of the cups of broth resting on a bench next to Walker. He picked it up and sipped it.

"Not bad."

Walker wanted to tell Lynch he was coming on like a bad Catskill comedian, but caught himself. Remembering their earlier encounters, he opted instead to see where Lynch was going.

"They tell you David Singleton didn't make it?" Lynch asked.

Walker nodded. He drank some broth, this time with more success.

"Some people in the department want you to go down on this one. Given your previous escapades, it sort of makes sense. You know, the out of control Pee-Eye goes off the end of the pier in a death dance with his client."

He paused and removed his hat to run his fingers through his iron-gray hair. Walker looked at Lynch but said nothing.

"Yes, we know Singleton was your client," Lynch continued. "We got that from Bledsoe's security."

Walker did not respond.

"But I told my guys to back off, said we need to hear your story."

Walker pulled the blanket tighter around him. He looked at Lynch and took a long sip of broth, which only brought on more shaking.

"All right," Walker managed through clattering teeth. Then, after summoning all his strength, he told Lynch about his first meeting with David Singleton, his efforts to find Allan, the discovery of the disc and its connection to the Cinema and Michaela. Pausing for sips of broth, and continuing in short bursts, he explained his theory of David Singleton's responsibility for both Quint's death and the assault on Michaela.

After about twenty minutes of Walker relating the details of the case, Lynch closed his notebook and looked at Walker.

"Is that everything?"

"No," Walker continued. He told Lynch about David Singleton's attempt to sell him on the idea that Allan was blackmailing him over the origins of Loon Lake Ventures, when the real reason lay deeper in the past, with the fire and their parents' deaths.

"I think he might have ridden out the exposure of the theft of his brother's ideas," Walker concluded. "After all, the man certainly was rich and powerful enough to massage the truth into whatever shape he wanted. But I don't think he would have been able to survive a full and complete airing of the arson death of his parents. He hired me to find Allan and then have Quint kill him. If along the way I managed to protect his secret about the stolen theories and codes, well, that was fine, too. But when Quint turned out to be a blackmailer, Singleton had to modify his plans."

"That's all very interesting," Lynch responded. "But you can't bring charges against a dead person. Plus, those damn highway flares looked like the real thing. Bledsoe's people had probable cause. No prosecutor would touch this."

"The disc should answer a lot of questions."

"Depends what was on it."

"David Singleton thought it was a record of the codes and equations he originally stole from Allan. I think it's something else entirely."

Walker told Lynch about Michaela's connection to the Israeli intelligence service and what he had seen in Allan's motel room.

Lynch reached into his pocket and brought out a plastic evidence bag containing the soggy, bent computer disc.

"I'm afraid it might not have survived its encounter with the bay."

"What about the gun—the silver automatic that Singleton took from Quint?
Did you find that in my jacket on the pier?"

"Yes, we got it."

"Run a ballistics test and it will match the slug that went into Quint."

"We intend to."

"Good."

"It was in your jacket, Walker. Not his."

"Christ, you don't think that I..." His voice trailed off.

"No," Lynch said. "But it is one more reason why we can't jump up and down and proclaim David Singleton a murderer. I may believe you, but that doesn't count for anything."

Walker got up and maneuvered himself to the window, the heavy blanket trailing behind him. He looked out into the parking lot, hoping to see the red Morgan. He had asked one of the firemen to call Linda when he first regained consciousness. Behind him, he heard Lynch speak softly.

"Let it go, Walker. It's over."

Walker turned back toward Lynch.

"The disc you found is a copy. The original still exists. I can get it."

Lynch stood up. He reached out to shake Walker's hand. Walker met his gaze.

"Go home now, Walker," Lynch said. "I don't believe you're guilty of anything more than lousy judgment in picking your clients. If you want to bring in the disc, fine. At best, it's going be a moral victory. Because, like I said, there's nobody left to prosecute."

Walker nodded, hesitantly accepting Lynch's handshake.

"Tell me something."

"What?"

"Did somebody hoist the homeland security flag up the old flag pole and tell you to back off?"

"Leave it be," Lynch said. "This whole thing is what my brother in law would call a walkaway."

"What the hell is that?"

"I'll tell you. Norm used to work as a Teamster on movie crews, and once they got the props and lights and cables set up properly, the crew would just *walk away* for coffee or cigarettes while the director and the actors—the folks making the really big money—dithered and talked about what to do. That's what a walkaway is."

Lynch lightly poked Walker on the shoulder with his closed fist and left the room. Walker asked for his clothes. When he put them on, he noticed they were not completely dry. Dressed, he stood shivering slightly in front of the window, his mind for the moment drained of thought and on idle, drained of thought. He waited for Linda and the Morgan to take him home.

Linda dropped him off and left, frowning and shaking her head when Walker asked her to stay. He stumbled into bed and slept the sleep of the dead for fifteen hours. A shaft of afternoon sunlight finally awakened him. Walker got up, went into the bathroom and used his razor to carve his face back to some semblance of its former self. Next, he took a long, indulgent needle-sharp shower, head bent forward resting on the cool tile as the water pounded against his neck.

Dried and dressed, Walker moved to the kitchen. He broke a half dozen eggs into a bowl, cut some green scallions, threw them in, added a few strips of Monterrey Jack cheese, poured everything into a skillet and using a wooden spoon, stirred and folded the omelet over high heat. He found a large plate, slid it onto the table, and served up the eggs with wheat toast. He sat down to eat.

The phone rang. Walker let the machine catch the call until he heard Delucca's voice. Walker punched the switch to activate the speakerphone.

"I'm here, Malcolm."

"You sound tired. I read the papers. Everything okay?"

"More or less."

"Seen the article in the *Chronicle* this morning?"

"Not yet." Walker took a bite of toast and chewed.

"Read it when you get a chance," the attorney continued. "The article makes it sound like you tried to rescue your client who was despondent over his brother's death."

Walker grimaced. The cover-up was already underway.

"Well, there is another version. Stay tuned."

"I will. I always enjoy the ongoing soap opera that is my favorite detective's life."

The attorney certainly was loosey-goosey this morning, Walker thought.

"I have good news, old buddy. Charging Ali as an adult is off the table. He made bail this morning."

"That's great, Malcolm."

"Tell me about it."

"I'll get back on the case this week."

"If you're up to it, great."

"I am."

Walker hung up and did the dishes, hoping Linda would call.

He went to his desk and called Toby Wolfson. He listened, scowling, as the math professor told him he hadn't cracked the code yet.

"Don't worry," Wolfson continued. "I have some of my best grad students on it."

"Thanks. Call me when you've got it."

Walker hung up. He had stalled as long as he could. He dialed Linda's number.

"Hey."

"Hello, Walker."

"Thanks for taking me home. I was in pieces."

"Not a problem."

Silence hummed on the line.

"Linda?"

"Yes?"

"I'd like to see you."

"Not now."

"How about the end of the day—up at the top of the Filbert Steps? Wine and a baguette?"

"Walker…"

"Don't disappear on me, Linda."

"All right. A half-hour. I'm busy later."

Walker entered a fragrant world of fresh cheese and Italian sausage hanging in clusters from the turn of the century ceiling, serving cases brimming with green and black olives, fresh focaccia bread, and marinated artichoke hearts. Walker crossed the worn plank floor to the number dispenser and watched as three men in green aprons efficiently filled orders. He just had time to pick out a bottle of Bardolino before his number was called.

Holding his purchases against his body with one arm, Walker left the store and ducked down the alley. A parking ticket fluttered lazily on his windshield wiper. Walker grabbed it, looked around, and was about to slide it under the window of a tan Dodge compact with a red spotlight on its dashboard when he realized he no longer had a wealthy client he could bill it to.

Walker walked down Columbus Avenue past sidewalk cafes crammed with citizens and tourists enjoying a day of bright sunshine in the Italian heart of the City. In recent years, many of the established shops and cafes had gone under as Asian businesses spread into the neighborhood from nearby Chinatown. There had been a minor outcry from residents about this invasion. Walker felt it merely added to the pulse of life in a city that never quite belonged to America in the first place.

Walker left Columbus and began the sharp climb up Filbert to the crest of Telegraph Hill. He passed what he guessed was a hundred-year-old Monterrey pine and hiked up a steep path to the open space beneath Coit Tower. Built to resemble a giant, fluted nozzle, the notoriously phallic landmark had been a gift to the City from Lillie Coit, a diminutive nineteenth century heiress who enjoyed riding with burly firemen as they hurried to conflagrations around the city.

Walker reached the top of the path and saw Linda twenty yards away, sitting on the lip of the parking lot looking out over the Bay. Her hair fell loosely at her shoulders. She wore a dark v-neck tee shirt, designer jeans, and a brushed suede jacket.

Walker sat down beside her and began to unwrap the sliced Prosciutto. Linda took a baguette and expertly split it down the middle using a Swiss Army knife she produced from her purse.

For several minutes, Linda and Walker ate without speaking. Linda put down her sandwich and stretched her arms above her head.

He opened the wine and offered it to her.

"A little early for me," Linda responded, looking quizzically at him.

"I guess..." He hesitated. "All right, I've been drinking more than usual lately."

He took a pull from the bottle and patted the cork back into place with the flat of his palm.

"Dammit, Walker," Linda began. "You don't have to play the dissolute detective with me."

"I wasn't playing anything."

"Oh, yes you were. You want me to feel sorry for you. I'm not playing that game."

"Things haven't been going exactly great lately," Walker blurted.

"I can imagine."

"What's that supposed to mean?"

"Nothing. Don't be so testy."

Walker gave Linda a quick summary of the roller coaster twists and turns of the Singleton case, concluding with his hopes for what the disc would reveal once it had been deciphered.

"So now you're hell bent to re-incarnate yourself as some kind of knight errant on a mission to restore the reputation of a crazy person."

"Damn it, Linda, it's not some melodrama. Crazy or not, the guy deserves to have his reputation restored."

Linda stared out at the Bay. She drew in a deep breath of crisp air.

"You don't get it, do you, Walker?"

"Get what?"

"Why do you think you found him, this missing brother, so easily?"

"Because I'm good at what I do? Because he wanted to be found? I know all that, Linda. I took Psychology back in the Pleistocene Age."

"I think you found him because you were looking for a part of yourself. The angry, lost part."

"Jesus, Linda."

"The part that's closed to me, Walker."

Walker tore bits of dough from the baguette and tossed them down the slope. Within seconds, three seagulls swooped down and devoured them.

"Rats with wings," Walker muttered.

Neither spoke for a long moment.

"How's Archie?"

"I think he misses you."

Linda laughed.

"Nice try, Walker."

"Hey, you're the one who said the little guy was a conscious, sentient being."

A silence settled over them for a moment.

"Are you seeing anyone?" Walker asked.

"Are you?"

"I asked first."

"I don't feel like answering that question, Walker."

"All right."

Another pause.

"What about you?"

"Not really."

"What's that supposed to mean?"

"It means…not really."

Walker threw some bread in the direction of the pigeons. There was more   fluttering and scrapping as the birds attacked the bread.

Linda turned to Walker.

"Did I ever tell you about the three-time rule, Walker?"

"Maybe. I can't remember."

"That's convenient." Linda picked at the baguette and threw a small piece of crust toward a pigeon hovering at the edge of the main group. "Well, it goes like this. The first time you sleep with someone, it's from passionate attraction. The second time is a kind of reality check to see if you really like it. The third time is to decide if you want to have a relationship."

"Who came up with this rule?"

"I did."

"Figures."

"So how many times have you slept with this new person, Walker?"

"There is no new person." Walker pulled the wine cork out and then patted it back in.

"So you made it to the third time." More statement than question.

"It wasn't like that at all," Walker responded, his voice sounding strained and strange to him. "There was an encounter. Nothing happened."

"I'm sorry for you, then."

Linda stood up and looked down at Walker.

"I have an appointment."

"Jesus Christ, Linda."

"I thought I could deal with your obstinacy, your knight errant with a mission attitude. Even this fierce identification with every loner, weird client who walks through the door had a certain charm. But not when it pushes me away, not when it becomes your whole world."

For perhaps the first time, Walker realized he should not take this woman for granted. He could easily lose her.

"Yes, of course," he responded in a quiet voice. "Can I give you a lift?"

Linda shook her head. "I have my car."

She brushed her lips across his cheek.

"Be careful, Walker. You could be heading for a major emotional flame-out."

"What do you mean?"

"The brother who was killed, the one whose reputation you want to clear? He may not be what you want him to be. The other brother may have it right and you could be wrong about what's on that disc."

Linda walked toward the parking lot. Walker—an only child who often had been lonely growing up—knew that Linda had hit home. Yes, Allan Singleton was indeed a brother, Walker conceded, a broken shard from the common Petrie dish we all swim in.

He stood up and went down the path past the big tree. Nearby, a homeless person rummaged in a trashcan; Walker gave him the bottle of Bardolino. The man smiled a ragged toothless grin of thanks and Walker walked down Montgomery Street towards his apartment.

CHAPTER TWENTY

Walker had been parked down the block from the Bakkrat home in the Excelsior District since 7:30 AM. He sat hunched over the wheel, steam rising from a thermos that he alternately sipped from and used to warm his hands. The neighboring modest stucco homes sweated condensation as the sun fought unsuccessfully to burn through the thick morning fog. Walker hoped to catch Hassan Bakkrat on his way to open his store, but no one had left the house in the past hour.

A gray-haired woman in a dark full-length dress, perhaps late seventies, opened the door. Walker wondered if she was the grandmother. From the doorway he heard an exchange in Arabic. Moments later, the elderly woman came out of the door and went down the steps with a small, folding shopping cart. Walker noticed she was wearing a beige head scarf but her face was uncovered. As soon as she turned the corner, he left his car and followed.

The woman went into a convenience market and emerged a short time later, pushing her shopping cart back towards the Bakkrat home. Walker intercepted her at the next corner.

"Forgive me," he began.

"Yes?" The voice was heavily accented but clear. Walker stared into deep brown eyes set in unlined face framed by the head scarf. Up close, she seemed younger than her years.

"I am working for Ali's attorney." He handed her his business card.

"Hassan is at home…I will take you to him."

"I wanted to speak with you first. Are you Mrs. Bakkrat?"

"I am Hassan's mother, Adriana Bakkrat."

Across the street, Walker noticed a bus kiosk, its glass walls etched and cut with jagged graffiti markings.

"Would you care to sit while we talk?"

The woman measured his expression before nodding her head once. Walker started across the street; the elderly woman's short, purposeful strides quickly over took his. Reaching the kiosk first, she carefully positioned her little cart to one side, took out a white handkerchief, spread it on the narrow bench, and sat down. Walker realized too late that the kiosk was smaller than it had seemed; he carefully lowered his large frame into the tight space next to her, ducking his head under the scalloped metal roof.

"Noor's boyfriend…Benjamin Navarro?" Walker began. "He told me that your granddaughter had crying fits. Difficultly sleeping. Is that true?"

Adriana Bakkrat looked sideways at Walker. Her cheek twitched slightly. "Yes, that's correct."

"This is difficult to talk about, Mrs. Bakkrat. But those are classic symptoms often associated with traumatic stress." No response. "Systematic, repeated stress."

Still, no response.

"Often as a result of childhood sexual abuse."

"Not in our family. Never." The voice was firm.

"Perhaps it was hidden. You might not have known."

"I was always there. I would have known."

Walker waited while a bus pulled to stop in front of them. A single teenage boy in loose baggy pants and a baseball cap got off.

"How often was Hassan with Noor before she came to San Francisco?"

"I do not know what you mean." Adriana Bakkrat's hand reached out for the shopping cart handle.

"In Palestine. When she was younger. Did she have her own room?"

"Yes." A pause. "She was of that age."

"Did Hassan, your son, spend time with her in that room? Perhaps to read stories to her? Perhaps with the door closed?"

Adriana Bakkrat stared at Walker for a long moment. Walker tried, without success, to read her expression. The older woman rose quickly.

"I must return to the house, Mr. Walker" she said, angling the cart in front of her. Walker watched her small figure turn the corner and slip out of sight.

He sat quietly for several minutes. This case was slipping past him like flip-cards in a child's nursery book. Having no coherent plan, he was ready to improvise. A bus hissed to a stop in front of him and he got up.

Walker crossed the street and approached the house. Steps rose at a steep angle from the sidewalk in a straight run to the front door. He paused to peer to the side of the stairs, imagining Ali, on a mission, clutching the silver automatic. *Whose mission?* Walker wondered. He admitted to himself that he, too, was on something of a mission. He rang the bell.

Hassan Bakkrat himself opened the door, slacks neatly pressed, shoes bright and polished, pulling on a wool sweater over his head. He extended his hand, presenting Walker with a tight smile.

"I am grateful for your help in getting Ali released on bail. Please come in."

Walker ignored Hassan's outstretched hand, entered the house, and closed the door behind him. "Don't thank me, Mr. Bakkrat," Walker replied. "Thank the attorney."

"May I get you some coffee?"

"No, thank you." Walker looked around. There were several doors leading off the hall. The grandmother stood like a statue in one of them.

"Is there some place we could talk without being disturbed?"

"Of course."

Bakkrat lead Walker to a small parlor in the front of the house. The furniture was large and overstuffed, out of scale with the room that featured a marble mantelpiece set above an old gas heater. When Bakkrat sat down in an upholstered easy chair, he suddenly appeared small and old. Walker seated himself on a cane chair facing Bakkrat and became aware of the fecund scent of raisins, or perhaps dates, steaming in a pot somewhere in the back of the home.

"I need to leave for the store in a half hour," Bakkrat explained. Hairline creases appeared at the corners of his mouth. "My cousin is opening for me, and I worry about him not knowing all the little things that have to be done. But I would be happy to assist you in any way I can."

"Mr. Bakkrat," Walker began, his voice calm, almost conversational. "The gun your son used to kill Noor belonged to his uncle—your brother, Mohammed."

"Are you certain?"

"Almost," Walker said, smiling pleasantly.

"Ali must have taken it from my brother," Hassan said, exhaling deeply. "I remember Mohammed told me it was missing."

"The problem with that is Ali was out of town at a tournament the weekend the gun was, as you say, missing."

Walker waited for a response. When none came, he plunged ahead. "I think you came into possession of the gun and gave it to Ali. With or without Mohammed's knowledge, I don't know that part. And right now, I don't particularly care."

He got up and in two steps was leaning over Bakkrat, in his face, his voice rising.

"What I do care is that you set this whole thing up. I care that you can sit back and let your son go to jail while you remain free as a bird."

Bakkrat drew his head back.

"It is outrageous that you would accuse me of such a thing."

Walker went over to the window and looked out. The fog hung on the street like a shroud. He wheeled back toward the room.

"Of course, you're no stranger to murder by proxy, are you, Mr. Bakkrat?"

"I have no idea what you're talking about."

"I'm talking about the betrayal of your brother Ahmed to the Israeli security forces."

"I did no such thing!" Bakkrat responded with vehemence. "My brother was killed by the Israelis during the *Infatada*."

Bakkrat glanced at the door and lowered his voice. "What does any of this have to do with the death of my daughter?"

"First of all, she's not your daughter. She was Ahmed's daughter."

"I raised Noor from the time she was ten years old. She was like a daughter to me."

Bakkrat stared at his hands for several long moments. His voice was barely audible when he spoke again.

"Where did you get this misinformation that I betrayed my brother?"

"From someone in a position to know."

"You have no idea—none at all."

Walker watched emotion, unreadable and unknowable, tug at the corners of
Bakkrat's mouth.

"The Israelis went through our village rounding up all the men. I was taken into a room where there was a field telephone operated by a battery. Wires were attached to my private parts. They knew my brother was a leader in the resistance. I told them just enough to make them stop."

"Enough to get him killed?"

"Why would I want to see my own brother dead?"

Walker took a deep breath.

"I believe you wanted Noor for yourself."

"What are you saying?"

"Something so terrified Noor that she threw herself sexually at the first man who showed her genuine affection. That man was Benjamin Navarro. He told me that Noor was extremely nervous, clingy, and had trouble sleeping. These are classic signs of post-traumatic stress, usually associated with systematic, long-term sexual abuse."

"How dare you say this in my house?"

"I don't know if it started before or after your brother's death," Walker went on. "But my guess is the abuse continued for some time. Probably for years. Then when Noor became old enough to have her own boyfriend, you panicked. Navarro became her life raft, her escape from you. You must've hated that."

Bakkrat was up and moving toward the door.

"I want you out of my house. Now."

"I know it might not be easy to prove," Walker continued, looking towards the door. "But eventually someone is going to remember something. Perhaps long walks in some particularly secluded part of the Palestinian countryside. Or an extra fifteen minutes you spent every night saying goodnight to Noor with the door to her bedroom locked. Not only will they remember—they will talk about it once they see that it can save your son from spending the rest of his life in prison."

Bakkrat's face was a battleground of emotions.

"Not only are you a pedophile, you are a moral coward." Walker's voice was sharp and knife-edged. "You convinced your son that the sister he loved was a whore who brought great dishonor to the family. You put the gun in his hand, Mr. Bakkrat."

Walker saw rage and anger boiling in Bakkrat now.

"I'm sure you thought that as a minor Ali would spend only a few years in jail. But I saw the look on your face when the attorney told you in his office that Ali could be tried as an adult. Your son could die or rot in jail. Unless of course you tell the truth."

Both men turned at the sound of the door behind them clicking open to reveal Ali, his eyes searching their faces for clues to what he had heard.

Walker moved past Ali to the front door. With his right hand on the knob, he turned back to the elder Bakkrat.

"It's still not too late to come forward. You can speak to the D.A. You can save your son."

"Leave my home." Bakkrat was shaking with emotion.
Ali stepped into the room.

"What is he talking about, father?"

Bakkrat placed a hand on Ali's chest, stopping his forward motion. For a moment, the thin boy and his tall father seemed to fuse into one person. Walker turned away and went out and down the steps to his car.

Walker entered the freeway at Ocean Avenue and headed downtown on autopilot. He barely noticed that the fog had finally lifted to the north—the minarets and towers of the city hovered in the distance like a disembodied Oz under what was now an achingly-clear cobalt blue sky. His neck muscles remained knotted and tight. The image of the father and son thrown awkwardly against each other seared itself into Walker's brain. The boy would now have to choose between his father and whatever version of the truth Walker could offer. Walker's parachuting into the situation with his hastily cobbled-together theory of the case could only bring more anguish to an already troubled family. He knew he was skating on thin ice, the truth dancing somewhere ahead of him, tantalizingly out of sight. On the other hand, Hassan Bakkrat was clearly on the defensive. Maybe his theory was correct and he would crack. He hoped to God he had done the right thing.

Walker looked at his watch. Earlier in the morning, after Walker had left for the Outer Mission district, Toby Wolfson left a message on his machine. Wolfson had deciphered the disk and wanted to meet him at Berkeley at noon. Walker had just twenty minutes to cross the bridge and meet the math professor in the café he had picked out. Walker pressed down hard on the accelerator and watched the MG's RPM needle jump. Several moments later, the Bay Bridge anchorage slid into view.

CHAPTER TWENTY

Walker parked on Shattuck Avenue a few blocks north of University Avenue, and walked the rest of the way to the café Toby Wolfson had designated for their meeting. To his left, the Berkeley flatlands sloped down to the bay several miles away. In the distance he could make out the Golden Gate, which at this hour acted like a wind tunnel, pushing tendrils of white fog across miles of choppy water through the Berkeley Marina and straight into Walker's face. He started to turn up his collar, only to remember he was wearing his Harris Tweed, and not his sturdy leather jacket. Thrusting his hands into his trouser pockets and leaning into the wind, he increased his pace.

The café was one of several in what had become known as the Gourmet Ghetto, home to *nouvelle cuisine* restaurants, bookstores and designer boutiques. As he entered, Walker noticed Wolfson seated in a corner hunched over the *Chronicle* sports section. Above him, several Ansel Adams posters of Yosemite and the California desert were spaced at regular intervals on the bare brick wall.

Wolfson looked up, smiled, and shoved the paper to one side. He was dressed in a tent-like Boston Celtics sweatshirt and his familiar baggy cargo pants.

Walker sat across from Wolfson. He noticed two empty bottles of Mexican beer next to the professor's elbow. A full glass nestled in one of his bear-like paws. Walker wondered how many he had already put away.

Wolfson answered Walker's unasked question.

"I've been sitting here for an hour, drinking and thinking about Allan," he blurted. "As you know, I never liked the guy all that much. Admired him, but never liked him. But still...dying the way he did, the papers talking about him like he was a terrorist. It got to me."

"The truth is a little more complicated," Walker responded. "As always."

Walker ordered a steam beer. He knew he had a long way to go before catching up with Wolfson.

Wolfson rifled the pockets of his cargo pants and came up with the disc, which he plunked down on the table. His fingers drummed a moment on the smooth surface before he spoke.

"My grad students cracked the encryption. Took a while, but they're good. From what you told me, I was expecting either to find a shopping list of purloined equations relating to his brother's company or else some trench coat secret memos and communications from intelligence agencies. Well, I was disappointed. I found neither. That is, at first I didn't. Allan was such a sly little fucker."

Walker's beer arrived and he sipped it directly from the bottle.

"Go on, I'm listening."

"I immediately saw that the disc contained a Diophantine equation—those are equations that can be expressed in terms of integers."

Walker looked lost.

"Just think numbers, okay?" Wolfson prompted.

"If you insist."

"The more I looked at it, the more familiar it seemed. Remember Allan's hero, Archimedes?"

"Sure."

"Well, the equation turned out to be one of Archimedes's classic problems. It was an equation for how many grains of sand can fit into the universe—"

"What?"

"Archimedes assumed that the universe could be measured. You could do that by filling it up with grains of sand. Bazillions of them. But you would need to invent a new number system to count them. This figure had to be large. The upper limit would be eight times ten to the sixteenth power. It would be, simply put, a formula for measuring the universe."

"All that was on the disc?"

"Allan hadn't solved it yet. It looked like he'd been working on it for some time. My guess is he carried the disc around with him for years, doing the calculations, working it out at little at a time."

Walker took a long sip of beer. "Nothing on there about David Singleton's company?"

"Nope. Sorry."

"Anything that Israeli Intelligence might be interested in?"

"Not unless they like to solve math problems, Walker."

"Any mention of a fire in 1957 in upstate New York?"

"Nope."

Walker sighed.

Wolfson wagged a thick finger at him.

"You're thinking he was crazy, right? Crazy like a fox, more like it. Archimedes's problem is a famous challenge in the world of mathematics—so much so that some years ago, a think tank in Boston offered a million-dollar prize to the person who could solve the equation. From what I can tell, Allan was getting very close."

"I wonder if David Singleton knew that."

"Why?"

"It would give him one hell of a motive for stealing the disc."

"How would he have known about it? And besides, from what you said about David Singleton, he wasn't exactly hurting for bread."

"Allan might have dropped a hint. Despite everything, he wanted his big brother to be proud of him." Walker paused and drank his beer. "Besides, for guys like Singleton, money is sometimes just a way of keeping score."

"Don't be depressed. You haven't heard everything yet."

Walker looked expectantly at Wolfson.

"Remember how I told you that Archimedes was a role model for Allan?"

Walker nodded.

"Well, here's where it gets really elegant," Wolfson continued. "Archimedes discovered that some of his fellow mathematicians were ripping off his theorems. They had their own version of peer review back then—when you worked out a new theorem, you would show it to your colleagues and they would vet it. Well, some of his so-called buddies were passing off his theorems as their own. So he came up with an ingenious solution to foil them. Take a guess what old Archimedes did."

"Wrote them in invisible ink?" Walker had an immediate sinking feeling.

"No, but you're on the right track. He simply booby-trapped them. When Archimedes sent out several theorems together in a package, he made sure that one or two of them had a mistake somewhere. That way when theorems with the mistake showed up he could expose the thief."

"What does this have to do with the disc?"

Wolfson's eyes sparkled with excitement. "When I was checking Allan's work on the theorem, I noticed a gap. It was an obvious blunder. Only another mathematician would see it, of course. Easily correctible. So when I fixed it, a line of integers suddenly rolled over into words. It looked like some kind of web address. Totally weird. What the hell was that doing there, I asked myself?"

"Go on."

"I got on the Internet and plugged in the address. It goes to something called Information Retrieval Systems. It looked like some kind of quasi-private intelligence-gathering group— Allan had found their back door entrance. He bookmarked a bunch of files dealing with prominent people like Ralph Nader, Jimmy Carter, as well as teachers, trade union activists, ordinary people like that. Do you have any idea what that might be about?"

"Yes, actually, I do." Walker fought to contain his growing excitement. He was not sure how much he wanted to share with Wolfson.

"I went back to Allan's Archimedes problem to see if he had buried any other messages. I found another 'error' that, when corrected, transformed into a complete log of the email traffic of this group. It showed that they were sending the files on the dissidents to a web site in Israel. And to some far out right wing groups right here in the U.S.A."

Walker realized Allan had done more than connect red threads—he had found hard evidence that the group had been disseminating a hit list. A way to neutralize dissidents without getting the government's hands dirty. Even if the right wing crazies only assassinated one person from the list, they hoped it would deter others in greater number from speaking out. A very insane hope, Walker knew, but he could see some operative in some obscure agency playing the thought out to a sub group of a sub group. *These are indeed the times we live in*, Walker thought.

"This blows my mind, Walker. Thinking of my old colleague, Allan Singleton, as a whistleblower. The guy's a fucking hero."

"Yes, he is," Walker answered. "If you can make me a copy, I'd like to give it to some folks who can get it to the media and the general public."

Walker thought of Michaela and the group she had mentioned. They would be able to verify if Allan had connected all the threads. He would have to find their identity and location, but he was, after all, an investigator.

"I have no problem with that," Wolfson responded. "My grad students can go over Allan's publications to see what parallels there are with the programs used by Bledsoe's companies. If they find any connections, we can go public with that, too. It could restore his reputation in the academic community."

"Thanks. I appreciate that."

"Hell, there might even be money to pay them to do the research."

"How so?"

"Allan was pretty far along on the Archimedes problem. What he had accomplished might be of interest to that think tank in Boston. It's worth me writing to them." Wolfson's palm covered the disc and he pocketed it. "I'd like to see the guy's name cleared."

Walker reached across the table to grab and shake Wolfson's upper arm.

"You're a good man."

Walker rose, thanked Wolfson, left some bills on the table, and headed to the street and his car.

Walker drove south on Shattuck to University Avenue where he stopped at a red light. Realizing that he had acquired a slight buzz from the beer, he forced himself to focus. Across the avenue, the sidewalk was momentarily awash with students on their way to and from the semester's first classes. Walker glimpsed scores of hopeful faces bobbing above a small tidal wave of new coats and sweaters. In the absence of traditional harbingers of seasonal change—Walker always missed crimson leaves and crisp fall air—he recognized that this ripple of plumage and color was one small marker of how the earth turned on the western lip of the continent.

His gaze returned to the students in their new fall clothes. The traffic light cycled from red to green. Walker made a right turn and pointed the car toward the freeway and home.

CHAPTER TWENTY-ONE

Three days later, the call came from Delucca as Walker sat sipping his morning coffee and reading the sports section. On the speakerphone, the lawyer's ebullient baritone reminded Walker of the rock singer the man had once been.

"Hassan Bakkrat walked into the deputy D.A.'s office two hours ago and admitted he obtained the gun for Ali," the lawyer's voice boomed, filling the apartment. "He described how he planted the idea in the kid's head to kill his sister...convinced him that it was his duty, that she was a disgrace, you know—the whole catastrophe. Apparently Hassan's mother—Ali's grandmother—had suspected the abuse scenario for some time, and when she heard you and Hassan arguing, everything came into focus. She was the one who convinced Hassan to turn himself in."

Walker lightly pounded one fist onto the table. "Yes!" he mouthed silently. To Delucca, he said, "I was out there on a wing and prayer, Malcolm."

"Yes, I know."

"What happens now?" Walker asked.

"Hassan will be charged with second degree murder and conspiracy. Because he has no previous criminal history, he was granted bail. The D.A. may be willing to deal on voluntary manslaughter for Ali."

"That's great, Malcolm."

"You're telling me. If somebody had said a month ago that would be on the table for Ali, I would've laughed."

"What're you going to do about your conflict of interest? You can't represent both Hassan and Ali?" Beneath the question lay another: who was going to pay the bills.

"I'm okay with that. My client has always been Ali, not Hassan. The court will appoint another attorney for Hassan. I spoke with his brother—the one with the import store—and he is going to pay for Ali's defense."

"That's great, Malcolm. Have you talked to Ali?"

"Not yet."

"Do you mind if I see him? I need to mend some fences."

"Go right ahead. But there's one small problem."

"What?"

"He's moved out of the family place. They don't know where he is."

Fog was everywhere by the time Walker arrived downtown. He eased the MG into a parking space in the alley behind the old government mint building at Fifth and Mission Streets. To the west, Walker saw half a dozen rivers of fog cascading like unchecked flumes over Twin Peaks. It had been worse twenty minutes ago, in the Excelsior District, when Walker spoke with Ali's grandmother on the steps of the Bakkrat home. He'd sensed Hassan Bakkrat's presence somewhere in the house— the woman's sad brown eyes cautioned him not to enter. After claiming not to know where Ali was staying, she stepped outside and, shutting the door behind her, pressed a scrap of paper into Walker's hand. On it she had scribbled her grandson's cell phone number.

"He's staying with a friend," she whispered, "somewhere south of Market," and went back inside.

Walker sat on the broad front steps of the mint and pulled out his cell phone. He'd been punching the same number at five-minute intervals on his drive from Ali's house, and there was little reason to expect that this effort would be any different. But this time, Ali's voice came on after the second ring.

"Ali? This is Walker. Your investigator." *Former investigator*, Walker reminded himself.

A pause.

"Yes. I know who you are."

"How are you doing?"

"I'm doing fine."

Walker heard a siren approaching, and covered his free ear.

"I thought we might get together for a cup of coffee—"

"What for?"

"Just to talk."

Walker watched a hook and ladder roar past on its way to Market Street.

"I don't feel like talking."

"You sure?"

"Yes, I'm sure. Besides, I'm busy right now."

As the fire truck turned right onto Market, the siren sound increased in volume on the phone. *Bingo*, Walker thought.

"I must go," Ali blurted. The connection was cut.

Walker put his phone away and headed toward Market. He turned right and walked toward the Powell Street cable car turnaround. Office workers and late afternoon suburban shoppers clogged the street. Walker entered the Flood Building—Sam Spade's fictional office and the real home to several of Walker's attorney clients—and came out at the back onto O'Farrell Street. He turned right and headed toward Market again, reasoning that this would be the most inconspicuous approach to the Powell Street cable car turnaround.

As he attempted to blend into a line of tourists waiting with docile patience to board a cable car, he realized he had forgotten how this simple nineteenth century solution to San Francisco's hilly topography had become a Disneyland ride. At the edge of the crowd, a vendor hawked *ALCATRAZ UNIVERSITY* sweatshirts, someone juggled silver tennis balls in the air next to a hat filled with a few coins and bills, and a bulky black man with a stubbly gray beard nursed startling sounds from a tenor saxophone.

Walker looked for the plainclothes cops usually assigned to the area to guard against pickpockets during tourist season, but failed to identify any likely candidates. He positioned himself behind the ticket kiosk. Toward the far end of the plaza, people on folding chairs faced each other at a long table. A hand would dart forward from time to time to pluck a chess piece, and in the same motion, sweep back to click a timer. Walker scanned the faces. Nothing. Then he became aware of a row of people standing behind the players and that was when he saw him. Ali stood behind a middle-aged black man in a threadbare sweater who was playing a young olive-skinned girl in a puffy down jacket, no more than sixteen years old, Walker thought. Ali's arms were crossed over his chest and he stood rigidly still, lips pursed, as he studied their play.

Walker threaded his way through the onlookers until he was standing next to Ali. Although the boy's eyes remained straight ahead, Walker sensed he was aware of his presence. The girl placed her opponent in check with a skillful knight move.

"She's good," Walker whispered.

"Yes, she is," Ali replied, his eyes darting to Walker's face and then back to the board.

"Do you know her?"

"Her name is Kamisha." Ali continued to avoid Walker's eyes. "She plays here a lot in the summer. She goes to Richard Burton High School."

The man moved out of check and Kamisha brought her second knight into play, continuing the pressure on her opponent's king.

Walker turned to face Ali.

"Can we go somewhere to talk?"

"Why?"

"How about closure? I think we both could use some."

Walker saw Ali hesitate. He nodded to Kamisha, flashed five fingers twice until she mouthed the letters "O.K." in response. He turned back to Walker.

"There's a burrito stand up the block."

Walker and Ali sat in the back of the narrow shop. Walker bought Ali a *carne asada* burrito and settled on a glass of freshly squeezed papaya juice for himself.

"You're not going to tell my family you found me, are you?" Ali asked between bites.

"It's none of my business."

Ali continued to chew. Walker wondered if it was the boy's first meal of the day.

"Your lawyer thinks there is a good chance you may go to the Youth Authority. Perhaps three years at most."

Ali looked down at his plate and then back up at Walker.

"And my father?"

"Considerably more. The exact amount will depend upon a judge or jury."

Walker reached out and placed his hand on Ali's arm.

"I am deeply sorry for you and for everything that has happened to your family."

Ali was silent, the muscles in his jaw working.

"I don't know if my father is capable of penance." He paused a long moment. "But it doesn't matter. In my mind, he is already dead. A walking dead person. He destroyed himself by what he has done."

"Perhaps over time he might come to see that."

"May he rot in the fires of hell!"

Walker was startled by the force behind the words.

"It is strange that I say this because I don't even believe in hell." Ali's voice returned to its familiar register. "Maybe I say it precisely because I do not believe in heaven, either."

Walker noticed that Ali's eyes were brimming and watery.

"The problem is there is not enough time in the world for me to do my own penance for what I did to my sister," Ali went on. "Every day I pray for her and for myself. But there will never be enough time."

Walker realized since he had last seen him, the young man he had first met weeks earlier had transited from late boyhood to the hard edges of maturity. It was as if Ali's adolescence was gone. An enveloping sadness crept over Walker.

Ali was the first to break the silence.

"I know Kamisha from school. Her family has a spare room they are letting me use." A small smile flickered at the edge of his mouth. "I am teaching her to play chess."

"She seems like a very nice person, Ali."

"She is."

Walker stood up and put down his drink. "You shouldn't keep her waiting."

He embraced Ali and turned away. His eyes were hot and smarting.

CHAPTER TWENTY-TWO

The first rain of the season came almost three weeks after Walker's meeting with Ali on Market Street. It was a hard, driving rain and Walker savored it. Sitting in his apartment, he could hear the Australian tree ferns and acacias rattle and shake outside his window. Gutters and downspouts released sheets of runoff into the streets, washing away the dry dust and pollen and city grime that had accumulated over the summer. Walker's spirit welcomed the change of season and the cleansing that came with it. He knew he might not feel the same way in December, when the rain would seem eternal and unending. But for now it was marvelous and new. East coast transplants like himself needed discrete seasons, Walker reminded himself. Endless summer was just that: endless.

He looked at his watch. Forty minutes before he had to be at the Double Play to meet Linda for their first "date" since the strained conversation on the grass next to Coit Tower. Walker had called the bar to make sure that it was indeed calamari night. He flipped on the TV to the local news and disappeared into his closet to rummage for fresh clothes. A pert and preppy female newscaster talked about storm drains overflowing, streams jumping their banks and automobile spinouts as if she were describing events of Biblical proportions. Walker wondered how she would survive a winter in Detroit.

He went to the refrigerator and plucked a bottle of steam beer from the back of the rack. As he was opening the top, a familiar image on the screen riveted his attention: Ali's street in the Outer Mission, the pale facades of the row houses bathed in red and white pulses of light from emergency vehicles, overlaid with the forced urgency of the voice of the studio announcer. *Tragedy struck for the second time in this quiet San Francisco neighborhood. The body of forty-eight year old Hassan Bakkrat was found earlier this evening, the victim of multiple stab wounds...*

Walker went to the TV and turned up the volume.

Police are said to be searching for his teenage son Ali, recently released on bail for the murder of his sister, Noor Bakkrat. Hassan Bakkrat was scheduled to be arraigned in Noor's death on a charge of conspiracy to commit second-degree murder. Police would like to question the son, who moved out of the home a month ago...

Walker watched as crime scene technicians wearing ponchos and raincoats moved in and out of the house. Yellow crime scene tape was strung across the steps. Walker let his head arc slowly down to the counter, where he rested his forehead for a long moment. He listened to sound of the rain beating on the window. Suddenly, his head snapped up. He moved quickly to the phone and called Linda.

She picked up immediately.

"I just heard. I was about to call you."

"Yes, I saw it. Listen, Linda..." Walker took the phone into his closet.

"Yes?"

"He didn't do it. I know he didn't." Walker knelt down and opened his gun case. He took out the .38 Detective Special and examined it.

"You can't possibly say that, Walker."

Walker stuck the gun in his belt and straightened up.

"I think I know who did it."

"Walker, you're being crazy again. Stop this. *Please.*"

"I know what I'm doing." He found his canvas Paris policeman's raincoat and slipped into it. "I can't talk now—I'll call you later."

"Walker—"

He hung up the phone, extinguished the lights, and went out the door.

Driven by the wind, a garbage can lid rattled crazily down the street. Rain stung Walker's face like birdshot.

The engine cranked over but refused to catch. Rain hammered the canvas top and thick rivulets of water streamed down the windshield inches from his face. Walker got out, lifted the bonnet, and removed the distributor cap. Using his shirt tail to wipe the inside of the cap as dry as he could, he then closed the bonnet and dove quickly back into the car. This time the engine caught fire immediately.

Walker dropped down the hill, made a left on Broadway and then right on Battery. The rain had snarled rush hour traffic and Walker cut over to the Embarcadero. Twenty minutes later, he found himself inching onto the clogged Harrison Street entrance to the freeway. Threading in and out of traffic for several miles, he found the logjam beginning to break finally at the split to Highway 280 and Daly City. Cars quickly filled all four southbound lanes and picked up speed, their rear tires spewing rooster tails of dirty water onto Walker's windshield. The resulting whiteout was as dangerous as a New England snowstorm. Walker made certain he gripped the wheel at the ten and two o'clock positions. Hitting a pothole in these conditions would be akin to taking a rocket-propelled grenade in Iraq.

Walker left the freeway and plunged into the streets of Daly City. Operating on memory and instinct, he navigated the maze of similar-sounding streets and found the garage with little difficulty. He parked a block away, shut down the engine, and turned off his headlights. Walker looked at his watch: ten minutes after seven. The garage appeared closed for the night, its bay doors rolled down, and there was no visible sign of any activity. In frustration, he banged his palm on the steering wheel.

Walker got out of the car and began to walk toward the garage. The wind whipped his raincoat at his knees and sheets of water beat on his shoulders. He clung fiercely to the old baseball cap he'd found in the back seat in order to keep it on his head. Walker peered through the glass upper sections of the bay doors and saw the hulks of car frames, some taped with brown butcher paper, waiting to be painted. The only operational vehicle was a cherry red Impala with dual exhaust pipes. Walker remembered the car from reading the police report of Noor's death. Benjamin had to be somewhere close.

Not sure what direction to take, he edged around the perimeter of the building. A soft glow of orange light drew his attention to an area behind the garage where derelict cars and parts of cars rested on the cracked tarmac. The light appeared to come from a porthole-shaped window in a small aluminum Air Stream trailer resting on cinder blocks in a weedy parking lot.

Knowing he would need back-up, Walker patted his pocket for his cell phone, only to remember that it had gone into the bay along with his leather jacket. He wondered how far he was from the nearest pay phone.

Walker moved carefully along the trailer's side until he came to the window. Inside, he saw Benjamin Navarro sitting at a small fold-down table, a bottle of Wild Turkey in front of him. He watched Navarro pour some of the whiskey into a greasy jelly jar, and gulp it down in a single swallow. Behind Navarro on a narrow bunk, hastily tossed clothes poked up from an open suitcase. The suitcase, Walker realized, made looking for a pay phone out of the question. He would have to confront Navarro alone. He moved to the door and tapped on it.

A moment later, Navarro opened the door a few inches and peered out. Navarro's eyes widened as he saw Walker and he tried to close the door, but Walker shouldered in past him. The air in the trailer was heavy with cigarette smoke, whiskey and sweat.

"Nobody invited you in," Navarro sneered, his voice slurred with whiskey. Navarro reached under the table and came up with a cell phone that he pointed at Walker like a weapon.

"Go ahead. Call them," Walker responded. "I'd love to hear you explain to the cops how you killed Hassan Bakkrat."

"You don't know what the hell you're talking about," Navarro said.

Navarro moved to the table and slumped into a chair. He put down the cell phone. His hand shook as he attempted to pour whiskey into his glass, sloshing some of it onto the table.

Walker, eying the cell phone, continued to lean against the open door jamb, letting rain and wind blow into the trailer. As if he had read Walker's mind, Navarro stored the cell phone under a pillow behind him. He stared hard at Walker, who let another ninety seconds pass in silence before he took a short step forward and kicked the door shut behind him. The small trailer shook and Walker saw the bottle and the glass jump sideways on the table. He moved quickly and sat down across from Navarro. Walker's left elbow and forearm rested lightly on the surface of the table while his right hand closed around the handle of the .38 under the table. He carefully drew the gun from his waistband and held it loosely against his thigh.

Navarro's fingers picked at the label on the whiskey bottle. He seemed buffeted by some inner struggle as if a part of him wanted to speak out.

The sound of the rain on the metal roof seemed even more harsh and amplified and Walker had to lean forward to hear when Navarro finally spoke in a low, constricted voice.

"Noor was the love of my life." A half-smile formed on his lips. "I know, looking at me, no one would believe that."

A gust of rain-driven wind blew the door open. It flapped back and forth for several moments. Both men ignored it.

"She never told me what he...did to her." Navarro's expression suddenly came apart, his facial muscles slack and loose as he fought back sobs.

"Jesus, all those years."

The rain continued to drum on the roof. Walker waited for Navarro to continue.

"You tell them I was gone when you got here, okay?" Navarro's eyes pleaded with Walker. "All I want is a half hour start. That's not a hell of a lot to ask."

Walker reflexively tightened his grip on the gun. His left arm remained relaxed, still resting on the table.

"Don't tell me the bastard didn't deserve to die," Navarro implored.

"I'm just a detective, not God."

The cords on Navarro's neck stood out like ropes. Walker saw his shoulder muscles suddenly contract as Navarro reached behind him and came up with a gleaming nine-inch hunting knife with a serrated edge.

Navarro swept the knife at Walker in a downward arc. The single discharge of the .38 in the small space was deafening. Navarro slid sideways from his chair, clutching his left thigh. The knifepoint rested deep in the table, vibrating and humming three inches from Walker's free arm. He grabbed the knife and attempted to pull it out. Navarro moved crab-like toward the door. The knife would not give up its purchase in the wood. Walker turned and saw that Navarro was gone.

Walker looked again at the knife. It was shiny and clean. But he knew tests could still reveal latent bloodstains. He spun around on his heel and went out the door.

The rain drove into Walker's face at a steep angle, forcing him to squint. Moving forward in a crouch, his gun out, Walker saw nothing ahead but blackness. He stumbled through ankle-deep puddles of water, falling once when his foot hit a section of a discarded transmission. He picked himself up and kept moving forward. Somewhere in front of him he heard the sound of one of the bay doors going up. Walker thought Navarro must be inside, probably getting his car. The new Impala, Walker thought, and stepped up his pace. He heard another door go up—or was it the first one being closed?

Walker circled around the back of the garage and came out on the street side. All the bay doors were closed and there no light from the interior. He approached a small door, tapped the glass section lightly with his gun butt and watched as it fell away like a miniature waterfall. Walker reached his hand in and turned the handle. In a moment, he was inside.

He looked up and saw a long curving roof supported by four high walls. For a moment, Walker thought he had entered a dirigible hanger and half expected to see the *Hindenburg* moored above him. The sound of the rain was louder than it had been inside the trailer. Walker ducked behind some hulking machinery and waited for his eyes to adjust to the semi-darkness.

Navarro was nowhere to be seen. Walker kept his eyes on the red Impala. Minutes passed. Walker looked at the machinery next to him. It appeared to be the main paint compressor. He picked up the paint wand and held it in both hands.

Walker heard the *click* of a car door opening and closing. Four in-line headlights snapped on, temporarily blinding him. Reflexively, Walker thumbed a switch on the wand and the compressor came to life with a rumbling hiss. The red car shot forward. Walker realized that Navarro was going to go over and through him and crash the roll up door in an attempt to reach the street. He leapt to one side and pointed the paint wand at the car's windshield. Thick chocolate-colored paint spread over the glass and Walker saw Navarro's hand go up as if to protect his face. Then there was a loud *boom* followed by crunching of metal and glass as the car swerved into the wall. Navarro's head came to rest on the steering wheel.

Walker went over to the car and carefully placed two fingers against Navarro's carotid artery. He felt a slow, thready pulse.

Walker went around opening doors and turning on lights. He found a phone in the office and called 911. He told them where to come and what they would find when they arrived.

CHAPTER TWENTY-THREE

Walker spent the next several hours answering questions from two Daly City homicide inspectors. As dawn began to break, and after several phone calls made to and from their counterparts in San Francisco and to Malcolm Delucca, Walker was escorted back to the City and the Hall of Justice, where he answered the same questions all over again. A San Francisco homicide detective Walker did not know—it was too early for Lynch, who worked the day watch—was polite and impersonal. It was agreed that the police would call off their dragnet for Ali, pending results of tests for latent blood on Navarro's knife.

It was mid morning when Walker took the elevator down from the fourth floor and walked through the metal detectors and out to the front steps. The rain had stopped hours earlier and the street and sidewalks appeared scoured and scrubbed. He saw the Morgan parked in a white passenger zone reserved for police vehicles. Linda stepped out of the car and opened the passenger door for Walker. The interior of the Morgan gave off an aroma of fresh coffee and bread. Linda ducked into the driver's seat and handed Walker a thermos of Peet's coffee and an Acme sourdough baguette. Walker took a sip and leaned forward to kiss Linda on the lips. She accepted the kiss without quite returning it, fired up the engine of the big red sports car and pulled out into traffic.

After a while, she turned to look at him and Walker saw a smile at the edges of her mouth flicker and die as it failed to reach her eyes.

"Yesterday evening was supposed to be our reconciliation dinner. Not murder and mayhem night."

"I know," he said softly. "I certainly didn't plan it that way."

More silence seeped into the space between them.

"You're not a violent person, Walker. But you seem to choose to live surrounded by violence."

Walker sighed. "It's what I do, Linda. You know that."

Linda pulled the car over and turned off the engine. They were at the foot of Potrero Hill near the docks. Huge cranes loomed in the distance. She turned to Walker.

"That's the problem. When I first met you, I guess I sort of liked the idea of you being a detective. It was interesting and sexy. Now I don't know any more."

"What don't you know?"

"I worry about your well-being. And not just the physical part."

Walker took a long sip of coffee and stared out the window.

"It goes beyond the violence. I've watched you on these last two cases. At first I thought it was just your normal obsessive behavior, shutting down everything else around you. But I realized that the cases had become so personal that they were defining who you were."

"I don't know how do the work any other way, Linda."

"The result is you shut me out. I feel sucked dry. Empty."

"You want me to say I'll try to do better in the future?"

"I don't *want* you to say anything." Linda's voice was tired.

Again, they were adrift in a pool of silence. Walker opened the car door and got out.

"What are you doing?"

"I need to walk."

Walker moved away from the car toward China Basin and the dry docks. The air was crisp and bright cumulus clouds stretched across the far horizon. He breathed deeply as he passed a crew working on a large container ship that rested on a latticework of stilts, its dull gray hull pocked and dappled with welding sparks falling in lazy drifts to the ground. He stopped and looked back at the Morgan. It wasn't right to leave Linda alone that way. But he'd needed to clear his head. He turned back and began to retrace his steps.

Walker watched the low-slung sports car pull away from the curb and head toward him. It continued almost a full block past him before its brake lights flared red as it came to a sharp halt. The Morgan sat there, its motor idling for several long moments. Then it did a slow, purposeful u-turn and began to come up behind him. Walker wondered if Linda would stop this time or pass him by. He was suddenly overcome by a soul-crushing weariness, and he thought about lying down in the middle of the road. In the end, he decided to stand and wait.

The Morgan continued down the street.

Walker found a pay phone and called a cab. He waited at home all day for Linda to call. When the phone failed to ring, he phoned her the following morning. Linda apologized for stranding him, but went on to say that she needed some emotional space. Towards the end of the conversation, they both promised to speak on the phone in a week. Somehow, it was a pledge Walker doubted either person would keep.

Peter Gessner is a licensed private investigator based in San Francisco. Born in New York City, he, like many of his generation who came of age personally and politically during the Vietnam War, migrated westward to San Francisco to reinvent himself. Too late for the Summer of Love, there was still plenty of time to fall in love with the city that had been home to an earlier author/detective. His first weeks were spent on a friend's couch devouring early paperback editions of Dashiell Hammett's stories, many with maps conveniently placed inside their back covers.

Gessner has been a Visiting Professor of Cinema at San Francisco State University and for one summer early in his career, he worked as a reporter for the *Village Voice*. He graduated with highest honors from Swarthmore College with Bachelor of Arts degree in English Literature and attended Yale Drama School. Prior to his arrival in California, Gessner had been an independent filmmaker; several of his documentaries that dealt with anti-war and labor themes received prizes at international film festivals.

His decision to become a private investigator was shaped in part by learning about a new breed of private detectives who emerged to prominence in San Francisco in the 1970's. Hal Lipset, Jack Palladino, Sandra Sutherland, Beverly Axelrod, and David Fetchheimer took on challenging cases of national significance ranging from the political nightmare of Watergate, the Jonestown massacre, and the high profile kidnapping of Patty Hearst. Their roots were not in the often narrow world of law enforcement, these men and women came from journalism, social work, and, in one notable case, single-parenthood.

After a yearlong hiatus from filmmaking during which he drove a taxi and nearly ruined his driving skills as well as his back, Gessner landed an apprenticeship with a local investigator who had trained with these investigators. Soon, he was working for some of them himself. Several more years down the road, he had his own PI license. Gessner's cases have included capital homicide and wrongful death investigations; sexual abuse of children by clergy; numerous police misconduct inquiries; an undercover inquiry into the harassment of a female member of a local ham radio club by male club officials; and the investigation of apparently racially-motivated death threats to a student at a prominent local private school. He does not own a gun.

A member of the California Association of Licensed Investigators, Gessner lives on the slope of a small hill on the southern edge of his adopted city. His daughter Francesca is a recent Stanford Law School graduate. *The Big Hello and the Long Goodbye* is Peter Gessner's debut novel, and is the first in a projected series featuring the San Francisco private eye "Walker."

Ps: If this detective is graced with a first name, we do not know it. This is, in part, a tribute to a similarly named lone protagonist played by actor Lee Marvin in John Boorman's classic 1967 film, "Point Blank." The two Walkers share one additional characteristic: a desire for justice in a flawed world tempered by a fierce desire to see things through to the end, whatever the cost.

Printed in the United States
85695LV00004B/57/A

9 781591 331995